Justice

And Other Short Erotic Tales

Justice

And Other Short Erotic Tales

To Amy,

a good friend and fellow gamer

Love, Peace, Hugs, Kisses, Whips & Chains,

Tammy Jo Eckhart

Published in the United States by Greenery Press, 3739 Balboa Ave. PMB 195, San Francisco, CA 94121.

http://www.bigrock.com/~greenery

ISBN 1-890159-14-X

Printed in Canada

AAF3182

Table of Contents

Still

IT SEEMS LIKE A SIMPLE TEST. JUST STRIP down and kneel there on my soft carpet and then be perfectly still. No movement, not even the slightest, and not a sound until I say "brickhouse." I've had to send a few applicants away at this point for asking "What?" Mine is a very clear order, a very simple test, which needs no further clarification.

But I never said it was easy.

One minute. That's how long I've crouched here in front of him, watching for any movement, listening for the slightest sound. He's made it further than half the others already. Most grin after a few seconds or sigh. One even winked at me. They were all told to leave immediately. I've never had to call on Frankie to help me, but she's waiting in the other room just in case.

After discussion over email, then at a local bar, I ask the special ones, the ones that seem sincere and clueful, over to my place. They are told that one final test must be passed before I'll accept them for training as my slave. A simple test that won't take more than ten minutes of their time.

Some think me too picky, too harsh, when dismissed from my realm or not even invited further than the bar door. I'd rather be picky than disappointed, aroused instead of frustrated, and I don't want to waste my time. It really is such a simple test. Just kneel there and be perfectly still.

Two minutes. I shift my weight a bit, but his eyes don't follow my movement. More than half those making it this far do, and so they are dismissed. Not this one. His eyes are the most common brown color, but their soft golden lashes and wide spacing makes them lovely. His hair, too, is that same golden tone that folks pay lavishly for at beauty salons.

His hair was how I found him when we met at my favorite bar, a place where my long flowing skirts and combat boots don't seem out of place among the would-be vamps and goths. His golden hair, though, definitely stood out among the dreary crowd, whose only color is often blood red.

And it's natural; he let me examine it closely that first meeting. My fleeting thought then was how much better it would be several inches longer in back. Now my hand clenches as I imagine the flaxen locks wrapped around my hand. "Don't go there," I remind myself silently. At least ten others have been here this long, but all were dismissed, so Frankie and I had to rent a movie and drown my frustration in ice cream.

Three minutes, the soft beep from my watch tells me. When I open the door to my dungeon, which I create by hanging dark curtains on the window and black sheets over the furniture, I always expect my would-be trainees to laugh. One did once; I guess he was expecting the same setup he'd been paying for, so I just slammed the door in his face. This one, though, just politely complimented me as I let him in.

Not even a comment on how I was dressed. Since the outfit is part of the test, I usually let those comments pass. Compared to the long skirts and shirts and combat boots, I'm sure my black lacy mini with matching shirt is a shock. I use this outfit now. I push my shoulders back so my breasts strain the shirt, and I part my knees so the mini is pulled taut at mid-thigh. Their eyes always glance down now.

Four minutes, my watch beeps. I blink, surprised that this one hasn't moved at all. I feel a drop of sweat start at the base of my scalp as my vision starts to blur. I decide to do something radical and stand up. I keep my thighs parted, the edge of my skirt just above his eye level. I hold my breath and watch closely. The drop of sweat slowly drips down to my eyebrow.

I turn at the sound behind me to find Frankie standing in the doorway between her room and the dungeon. She mouths her surprise and then chuckles as I wave her out of sight. Quickly I glance back down at him, but he hasn't moved.

This is strange. I'm feeling nervous, so I walk behind him. You'd think I'd never scened before the way my stomach is clenching. But I have, far too many times, with far too many disappointments, resulting in far too many broken hearts. This little test, this simple test, is my safety net. The most I ever get now is a bit pissed at wasting a few hours on the computer and a few bucks at the bar. And that hunger in my soul.

His hair is medium length, plaited into one braid down the back so it falls just to his shoulder blades. A simple rubber band holds it. It's just like I asked. At the edge of my mind a question forms that I can't deal with, so I crouch down behind him and move my lips right next to his ears.

"Getting tired yet?" I ask in a soft gentle voice. Nothing, not even a tug at his temples to indicate that he's trying to glance back at me.

At the five-minute beep, I touch his shoulders with the tips of my nails. Lightly, just barely making contact. Though he doesn't break position, his skin is damp and hot.

I blink as the drop of sweat falls onto my lashes. It is warm in here. As I stand up again I realize that my forehead isn't the only thing damp. I bite my lip hard, tasting blood, but at least the tingling that's started fades as a result. But I'm still hot.

I smile as I cross back in front of him. "Guess it's getting hot in here," I say as I undo the top button of my lace top. "I noticed you were sweating," I add as I unbutton another so that the tops of my breasts are exposed. "You know, Todd" – I say his name in the most sexy voice I can manage – "you've done so well already. Its just too bad that you can't have a better look." Then I unbutton the last two and let the lace fall to the floor.

Damn! Is there a gusher between my thighs now? He hasn't moved; he hasn't made one sound. The sweat, though, is visible on his face, and I'd swear he's blinking faster.

For a moment I see my training collar around his neck and my wonderfully worn pair of cuffs on his wrists. I wonder if he'll moan as I bite his lips when we kiss. I can almost feel his tongue on my nipples and my neck and I sigh.

Beep! The six-minute mark makes me shake. I realize my hands have wandered up to my breasts and neck of their own accord, and I quickly lower them. One final time I crouch in front of him, narrowing my eyes, looking for any sign of disobedience. Seeing none, I pick up my shirt and walk to the kitchen.

There I get a glass mostly of ice with just enough water to keep it from sticking to my lips and tongue. I stand there in the doorway watching him. The cold in my mouth isn't helping the fire under my skirt and the pounding of my heart.

My vision blurs a bit, and suddenly it's an ideal Sunday morning. As he lays the tray across my lap his blond hair falling over one shoulder catches the sunlight from the curtains he's opened. As I trace my fingers along his jaw and into his closest ear, teasing the folds, he sighs and turns so I have easier access.

"Did you eat?" I ask.

"No, Mistress," he whispers, the sunlight glinting off his lashes as he lowers his eyes. He moans and takes the other offered finger, covered in extra honey from my toast, eagerly into his mouth.

My entire body feels alive, warm, and safe as he works his tongue and lips until I am forced to withdraw or forget about breakfast all together. I pout as he whimpers and leans onto the edge of the bed.

The glass almost falls from my hand as my watch beeps again. Seven, the time I'd set in my mind. Only seven minutes? I frown at my trembling hand as I set the glass on the counter and clear my throat.

"Brickhouse," I say loudly, more to snap myself out than anything else.

He turns his head then and looks directly at me. After a few moments he speaks. "Did I do okay, Lydia?"

"Ah, yeah, you did fine," I say as I pull my shirt back on. "You can get up, please," I add as he just smiles at me. "And get dressed."

I make myself turn away as he pulls on his clothes. I know that scening right now would be the absolute worst thing to do at this moment. I need time to think; he needs time to think. A few days – heck, six days and it will be Friday. We can meet at the bar to talk about it then. I'll send him email.

"Lydia?" His voice brings me out of my sober thoughts. "It's been a pleasure," he says, when I walk him the couple of steps to the door and unlock it.

"It was very nice," I say, offering him my hand. If I weren't pressing my lips together so hard that they hurt I know my mouth would be falling open as he turns my hand and places one gentle kiss on the back.

He's a step out the door when I'm able to speak. "Todd?"

"Yes, Lydia?" He looks at me and suddenly those brown eyes seem so colorful.

"Do you regularly go to church or have family obligations on Sunday mornings?" I hear myself ask.

"No, not usually."

I wait a second, and his expression seems to urge me on. "Take me out to brunch tomorrow?"

"I'd be delighted to, Lydia," he says, lowering his eyes a little. After a silence he glances up with a grin. "Is eleven all right to pick you up?"

"Eleven would be fine, just fine," I say with a grin I'm sure is too goofy for words. I watch him walk down the hallway to the elevator, adding another, less starstruck smile for the trip before shutting the door on the hallway.

Resting my back against the metal frame I place one hand to my chest and concentrate on my speeding heart.

"Oh, no." Frankie's voice makes me jump, knocking my elbow into the door.

"Damn it, Frankie! Can't I get any kind of privacy?" I ask as I stomp into my own bedroom. I close the door on her laughter and pull my electric toy from his ready-to-use niche between my bed and bookcase.

It is such a simple test.

It just isn't easy ... for me.

As Is

THE PARKING ATTENDANTS DIDN'T BLINK when the motorcycle drove into the lot. Their customers, men in designer suits and women in silk dresses, were another matter. Those who came regularly just paused briefly at this odd sight. This lone buyer on wheels came to the auction about once a year. The newer clients turned and stared as the cycle pulled into a reserved space. You'd think they'd never seen a Harley in Florida.

The rider ignored the mutters and whispers that surrounded her as she locked up her bike and took off her helmet. One long auburn braid slid out and fell to her waist. She opened up the storage packs on the back end of the cycle and took out her leather saddle bags and tossed them along with some cash to one of the parking attendants.

The rider now brushed past the tiny crowd of hobnobbers outside the warehouse and entered another world. Outside, anyone passing would wonder at the rows and rows of convertibles, limos, and foreign sports cars all parked in front of an old warehouse. Inside the metal frame the walls were covered in silks and satins. Richly dressed tables with two chairs each lined the main floor at the center of the warehouse.

Two sales clerks dressed in matching business suits, a woman and a man, approached the biker with wide smiles. The woman spoke first. "Miss Donnerstein," she said. "We hope your trip was pleasant."

"Same as always," the biker replied evenly. "I'm hoping it will be more pleasant on the way back," she added with a glance toward the cages on the far side of the warehouse.

"I'm sure we could arrange for a limo or a helicopter," the man offered.

The biker looked at the man, then at the woman.

"He's a trainee," the woman replied quickly. She waved the man away and smiled at their client. "What exactly are you looking for?"

The biker and the house employee began walking toward the cages. "Another secretary," the biker said.

"Reggie didn't work out, then?" the sales clerk commented sadly. "Is there anything we can do to help you dispose of him?"

"I took care of it," the biker answered. She stopped at the first cage. "I want another boy, about the same size, and with secretarial skills."

The sales clerk looked at her computer clipboard for several seconds. "We only have three this time around. Girls are usually trained more in that area," she hinted, but received only a tired glare in response. "Two of these are close to Reggie's size."

The sales clerk led the biker to a cage with three male slaves inside. She pointed to the taller two, "Come forward," she ordered.

Both were about five foot ten in height and of slim build. One had a reddish tint to his blond hair; the other was black-haired. Both naked bodies were well tanned, their long hair pulled back at the neck.

"Drew," said the sales clerk, pulling the blond forward by the card which hung around his neck, "is thirty-six and has been with our service for a decade."

The biker barely looked at him as she shook her head.

"Adam," continued the sales clerk as the black-haired slave moved forward, "is twenty-eight and was born to two of our earlier sales."

The biker arched her eyebrows as she moved closer to the bars of the cage. "I didn't realize that you had been around that long," she commented as she read over the placard detailing the slave's skills and physical qualities. "He has allergies," she simply commented.

"Easily controlled by over-the-counter medication," the sales clerk replied immediately.

The biker reached through the bars, grabbed the slave's ponytail, and tilted his head back. His almond-shaped eyes regarded her seriously, with just a hint of fear in them and a whirl of desire. "How fast do you type?"

"70," the slave replied. His voice was rich and soft.

"Take dictation?" the biker continued, asking the questions she wanted to know to see if the placard lied. "Can you cook?"

The slave's eyes glanced down as he answered, "Basics."

The biker released the slave's hair. "Let's look at the girls," she stated.

All three slaves pressed against the bars of their cage as the biker left. Their eyes followed her in fear and longing. Embroidered on the back of her brown leather jacket was the word "FLAME." "I bet," sighed the one slave who had not been looked at because of his height.

The morning and the afternoon wore on as the customers gathered around the cages. When a gong was sounded, the clients all hurried back to the entrance of the warehouse, where they handed secret bids to the sales clerks.

"I hate this part," the reddish-blond male secretary stated as he sat down on the floor.

"What happens now?" the black-haired secretary asked as he remained standing by the bars of the cage.

"They'll come back tomorrow, and we'll see who, if anyone, we belong to," the short blond replied.

"Get some sleep," the taller blond recommended.

But the almond eyes stayed open for hours, looking toward the entrance. Several men had looked at him that day and even a few women. He pressed himself against the bars in the vain hopes that either the metal would help him orgasm or end the erection he'd built up over his days and nights here. It did neither.

The biker stopped in front of the cage and chuckled softly at the naked black-haired secretary who had fallen asleep on his knees by the cage door. She kicked the bars with her boot. "So anxious?" she asked as the slave hurried to his feet.

"You're very early!" yelled the same sales clerk who had accompanied the biker the day before across the warehouse as she sprinted to reach the cage where the male secretaries were kept. "Everyone get up now!" she ordered as she set her shoes on the floor and stepped into them.

"I want to head back soon," the biker replied.

"You," the sales clerk ordered as she pointed to the black-haired slave, "come out here and meet your new owner."

The black-haired secretary exited the cage as soon as the door was opened. He knelt down, pressing his forehead to her boots.

"Screw the formalities," the biker commanded as she stepped back. "Put these on," she said as she tossed a bag to the slave.

The slave stood up and unzipped the bag. Inside he found a pair of jeans, socks, boots, and a brown leather jacket with the word "SLAVE" embroidered on the back. As he pulled the clothing on he glanced at the biker and the sales clerk, who were signing some papers.

The jeans were skin-tight but felt soft and worn. Each knee had a hole, as did one of the back pockets. The socks seemed new, but the boots were definitely worn and had a D-ring attached to the inner side of each at the ankle. The jacket had a silk lining that seemed very out of place. The slave had just hooked the zipper at the bottom of the jacket when the biker returned. He tensed and held his body rigid as she grabbed his ponytail. A cry rose in his throat as he felt a knife slicing through his hair just above the band which held it back.

"Want it?" the biker asked as she held the dismembered ponytail in front of his face. At the slave's nod, she dropped it into his hands. "Follow me," she ordered as she hurried across the warehouse.

The slave shoved his hair into one of the front pockets of the jacket and jogged after the biker. Outside, the brisk air and the dim light of dawn urged him to zip the jacket up to his neck. He caught the lighter the biker tossed to him.

"I just have one of these on mornings when I ride," the rider explained as he lit her cigarette. "We all gotta have our vices, huh?"

The slave flipped the top of the lighter back down as he replied. "As you say, Ma'am."

"Keep it," the biker said when he tried to hand the lighter back. "Cool it with the Ma'am stuff," she instructed him as they walked toward her motorcycle. "I'm two years younger than you, I'll have you know."

She tossed him her extra helmet and took another drag on her cigarette as he stood with his mouth open but silent. "So what do you call me?" the biker demanded with a crocked grin.

The slave shook his head in confused silence as he brushed back his bangs, which now were no shorter than the rest of his hair.

"Gonna have to do something about that hair," the biker commented casually. "What do you call me? Oh, you could try," the biker offered as she crushed out the remains of her cigarette as she spoke, "My Queen, My Lady, She Whose Hand Controls My Fate." The biker paused and looked at the slave, who was staring at her seriously. "Or you could just try Mistress."

The slave closed his eyes and nodded. "Yes, Mistress. Thank you, Mistress," he said.

"Good boy, Adam," the biker told him as she slapped him on the back. "Ever been on a cycle?" she asked as she mounted her bike.

"No, Mistress," the slave replied as he eyed the machine uncomfortably.

"Put the helmet on and mount up behind me," the biker ordered as she started the engine. She placed her own helmet on, first stacking the braid up on top of her head. "Just straddle it and put your arms around me." As soon as the slave had his arms around her waist she tapped the back footrest with one heel. "Feet up here."

The slave released his hold around her waist as he heard a click. Looking down he saw that the odd D-ring on one of the boots was attached to the metal with a small chain and lock.

"Just until you get resigned to the fact that I own your ass now," the biker told him as their eyes met. "Put your arms around me and just move with me," she ordered as she turned back toward her front tire.

The slave bowed his body so he matched the biker's form. He shivered as the air whipped around him. The constant hum of the bike rattled his bones and made his legs and ass hunger. He had spent a week in that warehouse, ripped from his home, isolated from all contact, until the morning the customers came. All their probing and teasing had left him frustrated, but he was used to that. The vibrations of the bike, however, were new and alarming. He leaned his head closer to the biker's shoulder and moaned.

The biker chuckled as she felt his body pressed against hers, his cock hard and hot through the jeans. "Horny little bastard!" she teased. "We got hours to ride, boy, you best get yourself under control."

The slave simply moaned again and lifted his head up so he could focus on the road before them.

The slave groaned as he got off the bike and straightened out his legs. His cock and ass continued to throb as he walked around the bike slowly as directed, trying to get used to not having that constant humming between his legs. The chain on his right boot was still fastened only to the D-ring so it dragged along the parking lot pavement. He stopped in front of the bike and looked at his owner, then glanced back toward the fast food joint they'd stopped at.

The biker took off her own helmet and motioned for him to do the same. He paused for a second, then handed it to her. She pressed a twenty-dollar bill into his same hand.

"I want a half-pounder with extra cheese and only ketchup and mustard, extra large fries and extra large chocolate milkshake. You get whatever," the biker said as she dismounted. "I'll be here on the picnic table."

The slave pulled down the jacket as far as it would go as he entered the restaurant. He pulled up the collar and bowed his head as he waited in line. He felt so exposed here, so displayed to the world. "May I take your order?" the cashier asked making him jump.

"Yes, please. A half-pounder and a quarter-pounder, both with extra cheese, just ketchup and mustard. Two extra large fries, a chocolate milkshake, the biggest you have, and a medium soda."

"What kind?" the cashier asked.

"What kind?" Adam repeated.

"Yeah, do you want a cola, diet cola, orange..."

"Diet," Adam replied. He handed the cashier the twenty and collected the change. As he moved over to the pickup counter he felt several pairs of eyes on him. A couple of men dressed in cowboy hats and boots took a couple of steps closer to him.

"Sir, your order," the pickup boy interrupted the slave's worries.

The biker watched as her property maneuvered past the small group of truck drivers who were harassing him. When a particularly nasty looking fat man grabbed the slave's hand the biker cleared her throat and yelled, "He ain't for you, boys! Let my man pass!"

The truckers laughed but moved aside as the slave hurried down the hill to the picnic table where the biker sat. "Mistress, I'm sorry," the slave began.

"I can see, I got two eyes," the biker replied as she took the large bag of take-out from him. She held out her hand and nodded when he placed her change in it. "Now the secretary part of your job can officially begin," she stated as she took a computer pad from one of her saddle bags.

The slave turned the unit on, and stood at attention.

"File is Expenses, subheading Daily. Enter what you just spent," the biker ordered as she unpacked their lunch.

Expertly the slave called up the files. "What the?" he said as he found the day's worksheet and the price she'd paid for him.

"I wanted to make sure I got you," was the biker's only comment. "Hurry up there, boy; I want to put a lot of miles behind us before we stop for the night."

The slave quickly entered the figures and closed out the files.

"I'll take it; now sit down and eat," the biker commanded with a tap of her boot on the bench.

The biker looked down from her seat on the table top and smiled as the slave wolfed down his food. She shrugged when he glanced up at her self-consciously. "When did you last eat?"

"A couple of days ago, Mistress," the slave replied as he set the last bit of his burger on its wrapper.

"Why would they do that?" the biker asked, a twinkle in her eyes.

The erection that had been destroyed by the crowd in the restaurant now stirred at the humiliating question. Adam bowed his head and answered softly. "To make sure we were clean for inspection by the buyers."

Silence hung in the air for several seconds. "You better finish eating," the biker suddenly said, "When I'm ready to go, we go."

The slave glanced around him anxiously as he stood at the urinal. One of the two men who had been in the john when he entered had left, but the other, one of the truckers who had harassed him earlier, stood off to the side watching him. His cock, hard from her question and the nearness of her body, made pissing difficult.

"Need a little help?" the harsh voice of the trucker asked.

The slave forced a stream to gush forth out of fear and shook his head. "No, thanks." He zipped up and headed to the sink.

The trucker moved behind him and slipped his hands onto his ass. "So, is that jacket correct, slave?" the trucker whispered; his breath smelled of alcohol as he leaned over the frightened man's shoulder.

Adam thrust back with his elbow, catching the trucker in his rib cage. The slave sprinted from the restroom, his hands still wet, and fled down the hill to the biker. Without a word, he took the helmet, hopped on the back of the bike and met his owner's inquiring eyes. "Please go," he begged as he fastened the helmet under his chin.

The biker waited to press the issue until they were out of sight of the restaurant. "So, what happened in the john?" she asked as they pulled over.

The slave slid back to the end of the seat and took a deep breath. "One of the truckers just wanted a little action, Mistress."

The biker unclipped one end of the chain on his right boot as she spoke, "And?"

"I hit him and ran out to you, Mistress."

"You could have used him to get away," the biker said as she held the chain to the footrest but didn't fasten it.

"Away from what, Mistress?" the slave replied diplomatically. His face fell when she fastened the chain to the bike anyway.

"Hang on. I want to clear another one hundred miles before we stop tonight," the biker explained.

The slave set the duffel bags down on the bed in the hotel. He stood quietly as the biker looked around the room then tossed the manager a few bills. The room was clean and solid, a good deal for the price. A color TV, no cable, stood by the windows. A simple table and two chairs were next to it. One queen-size bed occupied the bulk of the tiny room leaving barely enough room to get into the bathroom.

"Here," the biker said as she tossed the slave the complimentary ice bucket. "The ice is down the hall then one flight down."

The slave thanked his god that the hotel was mostly empty as he hurried to collect the ice. He entered the hotel room and locked the door behind him. The sound of water told him that she must be in the bathroom; there were few other places to hide in the tiny room.

"The boots, the socks, and the jacket come off now!" the biker's voice called from the direction of the restroom. "Money's in my jacket! Order us a large pepperoni pizza and two Cokes!"

The slave went to the phone first and dialed the pizza number on the hotel ad sheet by it. He removed his boots and socks and placed them back into the duffel bag she had handed him back at the warehouse. He hung his jacket up next to hers and took her wallet from her inner pocket. A whistle escaped his mouth as he looked at all the twenties inside. He took out one, and replaced the wallet.

He went to the window and looked out, waiting for the pizza delivery. His body was starting to ache from all the riding; his legs felt like they wouldn't close completely. He closed his eyes and remembered the feeling of the trucker's hands on his ass.

"You look nice in that sunset," the biker's voice spoke making him turn around in embarrassment. He blinked at her. She wore a sleep shirt with the words "bitch on wheels" on the front and a pair of torn leggings; around her head was wrapped a white towel. She removed the towel, and her wet, free locks of hair fell down. "Get the comb in my duffel bag."

The slave stuck the money into the hole-free back pocket of his jeans and went to the saddle bag which had not contained the duffel bag. He took out the large pink comb. Kneeling in front of her, head bowed, he offered it to her on open palms.

"You're going to comb it out, boy," the biker ordered as she sat down on the edge of the bed.

The slave stood up. Slowly, placing his hand on her hair to keep it from pulling so harshly, he ran the comb through it. Silky, thick, curling already in his fingers, her hair parted easily. He ran the comb over and over, smiling when she sighed and relaxed a bit.

"What's your name again?" the biker asked.

"Adam, Mistress."

"Adam," the biker repeated. "I could change it, you know."

The slave didn't pause as he agreed, "As it pleases you, Mistress."

"Adam. I think it will do," the biker stated. She tilted her head forward as the slave combed through the very ends of her hair. "Theresa Amanda Donnerstein," she said suddenly. "That's my name. Memorize it, Adam."

The slave continued combing as he thought about her name. He nodded, then shook his head, sure that the Donnersteins who had come to his previous owner's home for parties had no relationship to this biker. He noted that her neck muscles still looked tense. "May I rub your shoulders, Mistress?" he asked softly.

She nodded and moved her hair over one shoulder. "Anticipating my needs already, boy?"

"I'll try, Mistress," he replied as he blew warm air into his hands. He placed these gently on her shoulders and began to massage gently. After a few seconds, he lost himself in her shoulders, the material of her sleep shirt and the heat from her skin melting into his palms. His hands trembled as he moved his hand to her shoulder blades and continued.

"Adam," she said. Theresa turned toward him and repeated his name, "Adam."

"Yes, Mistress?" the slave replied as he pulled his hands back behind his back.

"The door. I think our pizza is here," she said as she took the comb from the night stand and began parting her hair into three plaits.

The slave stood up at the next ring of the doorbell and sprinted to the door. "Hi; it's fifteen dollars, right?" he asked as he took the pizza and the soda cans.

"That's the total with tax," the kid said.

"And the tip?" Adam asked as he turned toward the bed and opened the door wider.

Theresa stood up and walked to the door. She stepped just in front of her slave and took the twenty from his hand. "You have a choice," she said to the pizza boy, "you can have a five dollar tip or you can have him."

The pizza boy looked at the woman with a grin. "What do you mean, lady?"

"He's real good," Theresa replied as she caressed the crotch of Adam's jeans with her hand that held the twenty dollar bill.

The pizza boy grinned nervously. "Is this for real?" he asked the man.

"Yes, sir. Just tell me what you want," Adam said in a monotone.

"I think I'll just take the money," the pizza boy said as he held up his hands. "I'm not into this kinky shit."

"Thanks for delivering our pizza," Theresa said as she handed the pizza boy the twenty. She watched the pizza boy run down the hall, the stairs, and out to the parking lot where his car waited. "Too bad. I was hoping to see if the placard was correct about your cock sucking talents," she commented as she shut the door.

The slave gasped as her hand returned to his crotch. "You wanted to do it, didn't you?" she asked, locking the door with her other hand.

Trapped with the hot pizza box in his hands and his groin in hers, he merely nodded.

"So," Theresa continued as she moved to the table, pulling him by the balls after her. "They didn't let you eat for a few days. I assume they limited your sexual activities as well."

"Yes, Mistress," he replied, his balls pulsing in her hand. She looked at him intently, so he continued. "For a week, we were denied any physical contact with the trainers, the auctioneer, or the other slaves. It made us," he paused, his face red. "It made us very responsive to the buyers."

She squeezed his balls slowly until he closed his eyes in pain and desire. "Let's eat. I'm starving."

Adam looked at the last piece of pizza in the box, which sat on one of the chairs so he could reach it from where he sat on the floor.

"You want it?" Theresa asked as she finished her soda. "I'm not hungry, so go ahead."

"Thank you, Mistress," he replied as he took it.

"Eat it like it turns you on," she ordered with a slight grin on her face.

Adam paused with the tip of the pizza in front of his lips. He looked up at the biker as she leaned back in her chair and smiled down at him.

"You understood what I said. Do it."

He rose to his knees and positioned his body as he would for a master's penis. Tilting back his head, he held the pizza slice in both hands, curving the sides inward. He opened his mouth, keeping his lips over his teeth and began sliding the slice back and forth along his tongue. At his owner's nod, he took the slice deep within his throat where he worked his muscles. Several times he repeated deep throating the pizza then pulling it out slightly with a moan, finding that his humiliation forced arousal upon him once more.

Theresa reached out with one of her bare feet and shoved the slave's chest lightly. "Cut it out and just eat it," she giggled.

"Yes, Mistress," Adam replied as he took the pizza slice out of his mouth. The crust was soggy with his spit, but he gobbled it down quickly.

Without orders he cleaned up the table, then stood at the foot of the bed, looking at his mistress as she watched TV. "Go brush your teeth; there's a travel case in your side of the saddle bags," she ordered as she flipped channels idly.

Once inside the bathroom, he was able to look at himself for the first time in a week. His cheeks looked a little thin, but if she continued to feed him like this, he'd have to do some serious pushups. He washed his face first, then brushed his teeth thoroughly and gargled with the mouthwash which had also been in the travel pack. Finally he used the toilet, then double checked his face.

When he emerged from the bathroom he found his owner sitting cross-legged on the bed with the saddle bags next to her. He had left the travel bag in the bathroom, but the look in her eyes drew him to his knees by the bed in front of her.

She ran her fingers through his bangs, pushing them behind his ears. "Got to get this cut somewhere tomorrow," she muttered. Her hands now traced his jaw line over and over. "Electrolysis?"

"Yes, Mistress," he replied, his voice already husky with his own desire.

Theresa leaned on the edge of the bed, so her hands could reach all of him easily. She ran her hands down his chest, grinning as he straightened his back as much as he could to allow her complete access. "I'm told that you were born a slave, Adam."

"Yes, Mistress," he affirmed.

"But slavery is outlawed in the US." Theresa pulled the button loose from his jeans. "So that's not the truth, is it?"

Adam pushed his crotch forward in response to her tug at his zipper. "Mistress? Oh, my parents were some of the first members of the Auction House. I was raised as an equal in my master's house, well, like the children of his house servants at least, but when I turned sixteen he threw me a birthday party. He gave me a choice – I could take some money and move to a boarding school, then go to college; he'd pay for it all. Or I could get down on the floor and crawl to him and become his property. It felt right, so I crawled across the floor."

"Take these things off," Theresa ordered with a tiny fondle of his cock as it poked up through the open jeans. She sat up on her elbows and watched as he slipped out of the jeans, folded them and then knelt as before. "That's kind of sick. Sixteen, I mean, to make that kind of decision."

"If you say so, Mistress," the slave replied sadly. He looked up when she lifted his chin with one finger.

"So who's Asian? Your mother or your father?"

"My mother, Mistress," he said. He leaned toward the bed as she drew back slowly.

Theresa sat up on her knees and opened her side of the saddle bags. She sat a black leather bag on the bed and tossed the saddle bags to the floor. "I want to see what I bought, boy."

Adam's body trembled in hope as he looked at the leather bag. He licked his lips as she took a large phallus from it and held it in front of him.

"You want to please me, don't you, boy?" she teased as she moved the phallus closer to him.

"Yes, Mistress," he said as he wet his lips more.

"I'm going to hold it, and you're going to demonstrate your skills," Theresa ordered in a whisper.

He opened his mouth and slid his lips around the phallus. He glanced up at her as he bobbed his head up and down.

"Make it good and wet, cocksucker, because it's all the lube you're going to get," she hissed.

Almost reflexively his mouth watered and the spit started dripping from the sides of his mouth. He rolled his tongue over every centimeter of the phallus. He followed it as she lowered it to the floor then raised it up high so he had to strain to get it. "Please," he begged as she withdrew it from his reach.

"On your hand and knees, ass high," Theresa ordered as she hopped off the bed. She crouched behind him. "Part those cheeks," she ordered with a playful slap to them.

Adam leaned forward so he could rest his head against the bed and reached back with both hands. He felt her fingers around his as she closed one of his hands around the base of the phallus.

"Do it, boy, and make it a good show," she ordered as she sat back.

This was familiar to him; his master's son had taken him under his wing and had even taken him to college. Often, the young master had been tired and had ordered Adam to impale himself on either his cock, a friend's cock, or an artificial one. Now the slave pressed the tip to his hole and pushed it in slowly, rocking his hips back eagerly and sighing open-mouthed so the biker would be entertained.

Once inside, he let it rest for a moment, then slid it out until only the tip was hidden by his pink folds. As he slid it in and out, each time not pulling it out quite so far and pushing it in as far as he could, his back arched back so that his ass muscles could thrust and clench in full view. His breath came in gasps; his moans grew louder as he pressed his cheek into the bed.

"Are you hard?" Theresa asked huskily. The slave looked up at her, his eyes glazed over with his desire. "Let me see," she ordered as she gripped his hair and tilted his head back.

Adam leaned back, forcing his ass lower and causing his thrusts to angle sharply so he could tilt his groin toward her. He moaned as she wrapped one hand around his stiff, red pole and stroked it slowly just once.

"Stop," she whispered then smiled when he groaned and let his hand fall to the floor. His hips still pumped, so she tightened her grip on his hair and used her other hand to slap his face.

Adam's eyes burst open, cleared by the pain. He held his breath and body still as he watched the biker shake her head. His voice broke as she slapped his face in the opposite direction. In his years of service to the master and then the young master, he had never been slapped. Tears welled up in his eyes as he waited for another blow.

Theresa released her hold on his hair and used that hand to smooth it down, petting him gently as his body shook from the punishment. "When I give an order it is to be obeyed, slave. Do you understand me?"

"Yes, Mistress," he said, but frowned in confusion.

"No, you don't," she said as her fingers pulled his hair tightly again and forced his face up.

"Please, Mistress," he begged, his words were whispers as his dark eyes fastened on hers. "I thought I had obeyed."

The biker tilted her head then slapped him twice, once in each direction, before pulling his face toward her again. "Your hips were still humping that cock. You didn't obey," she stated.

"Yes, Mistress, I understand now. Thank you, Mistress," he replied, tears streaming down his face. He gasped as her hand touched his face and caressed the heat raised there by her slaps.

"Take it out and wash it," Theresa said as she let his head fall to the bed and then got up onto the bed herself. She glanced once at his form in the bathroom as he soaped and rinsed the fake phallus carefully. But when he knelt next to the bed and offered it to her on open palms, head bowed in shame, she reached back without a look and took it. She slipped it into her bag.

"Up here," she ordered as she turned the TV on and flipped to a sitcom.

Adam climbed onto the bed, then resumed his position. His thighs were separated so that his balls hung down, as did his shrinking cock. His toes pushed his ass up so that the cheeks were spread, his palms rested on his thighs.

"Grab your elbows behind your back," Theresa instructed with a tiny glance at him to make sure he complied. "Your back doesn't have to be so straight, boy. You're up here to amuse me, not kneeling formally on the floor now."

"Yes, Mistress; thank you," he whispered as he let his shoulders slump a bit. The position of his arms and legs, however, kept his chest and groin fully displayed. From under his bangs his eyes moved from the biker to the TV and back again as the minutes passed. When his eyes focused on the dim-witted blonde on TV he felt a cool touch on his inner thigh. Looking down he saw her short nails carve four red trails in his skin as the coolness was replaced with the fire of pain.

"You ever just served as a toy for your old master?" Theresa asked as she continued to drag her fingernails up and down one inner thigh for three round trips. "I mean, you ever just been ordered to react and let him do what he wanted to you?"

Adam moaned as her hand jumped to his other thigh and repeated the carving. "Yes, Mistress; it was very hard to do," he stated as his fingers twitched, aching to grab the blanket for strength.

"You ever been slapped before?" she asked and stopped her hand on top of his once more stiff cock.

"No, Mistress," Adam admitted softly. He turned his head as her other hand directed but otherwise remained still. Her eyes, a combination of brown, gold, and green, stared into his soul as she spoke.

"You didn't like it, did you, slave?"

"No, Mistress," he squeaked, his voice quivered as his body received mixed signals from the hand holding his chin firmly and the other stroking his erection just slightly.

"Then that will be your standard punishment from now on. My last boy had no discipline. He was a disgrace to the Auction House and his former owner," Theresa said very slowly and clearly. "I had him blacklisted, he won't be sold or be allowed to become a buyer for the rest of his life. So, if my hand gets tired from helping you remember how to obey, I'll do the same to you."

Adam's eyes widened in terror. Sure, he had an associate degree in secretarial management, but no money and no connections outside the world of the Auction House. For a slave like himself, one of the second generation, to be blacklisted in the Auction House would be equivalent to death. His mouth was dry as he spoke. "I will be good, Mistress; I," he started to promise then turned his head suddenly to one side and let out a loud sneeze.

Theresa's eyes widened and her mouth curled, and then a deep laugh bubbled up from her stomach. She threw back her head and clapped her hands several times as his first sneeze was followed by no less than three more of decreasing volume.

"Mistress, I'm so sorry," Adam begged as he sniffed and turned back toward her when his nose stopped tickling.

"In your," Theresa gasped as she tried to control her laughter. After a moment she sighed and grinned at his flushed and frightened face. "In your travel pack you'll find your allergy pills. They gave them to me at the Auction House. Go take one before we go to bed," she ordered as she flipped off the TV.

Adam released his arms and slipped off the side of the bed. He hurried to the bathroom and took two of his regular medication.

"You should make a note of that on the computer calendar, filed under daily schedule, when you put in the pizza expense," Theresa ordered as she packed the black bag inside the saddle bags and dumped them onto the floor.

Adam returned to find her taking off her leggings. He returned his travel pack to his duffel bag, then reached for the computer in the saddle bags. As he quickly entered all the information, setting his medication reminders for every day and adding a beep for a audible reminder, the biker turned down her sheets and crawled under them.

Theresa smiled as her slave stood by her bed and informed her that all was put away and accounted for. "You want to sleep outside the door and watch for robbers?" she asked with a grin and a twinkle in her eyes.

"As you wish, Mistress," Adam replied, but his nervous swallow betrayed his true feelings.

"Nah, this place is safe enough," Theresa relented with a giggle. "There's a pillow and a blanket at the foot for you. Good night, Adam. Remember everything you learned today, slave, because I don't have time to repeat it tomorrow. I want to get across another state."

"Yes, Mistress," he whispered as he knelt down by her bed. He bit his lip as he looked at her peaceful face. When her eyes reopened and frowned at him, he bowed his head and mumbled good wishes. At the foot of the bed he lay down, his arm cradling the pillow while his head rested on his arm. The blanket he likewise pulled mostly to his front to cuddle. As his eyes closed, he almost felt the young master's body next to his.

Adam opened his eyes slowly as the sunlight from the open curtain hit his face. He reached for the silk pillows he was used to but instead found only the plain one and the matted carpet underneath. His hands registered the feeling of the hotel blanket as he remembered where he was. Pushing himself up onto his knees he spotted the biker pulling on her boots. She was already dressed except for those and her jacket. When she looked at him with a frown, Adam quickly rose.

"Not quite the greeting I was expecting, you horny dog," Theresa commented as his cock bounced.

Adam moved his hands in front of his groin and mumbled an apology. "Good morning, Mistress," he added with a blush.

"Go hop in the bathroom and get ready. Hurry," she added, "I want to get going here."

Once done with the sink and toilet, the slave looked through his duffel bag for clean clothing. Inside, however, were still the same socks, a cock ring, and nothing else. He swallowed and ducked outside to fetch his jeans, which were still lying by the bed. Using a damp washcloth he tried to clean up the inside of the jeans, where the cycle and the previous night had caused him to leak. When the biker called from the other room he sighed and pulled the jeans on, adjusting the wet spot as best he could.

Theresa ignored the obvious mark on her slave's jeans as he emerged, carrying his duffel bag. "You drink coffee for breakfast?" she asked.

"If that's allowed, Mistress," Adam replied politely as he laced up his boots.

"You have good manners," the biker replied. She waited until he had his jacket on to pull out a cigarette. After a moment of fumbling in his pocket for the lighter, he lit it silently. "One a day," she said, perhaps more as a reminder to herself than him.

Adam carried the saddle bags to the cycle as the biker paid the bill in the office. He smiled when she returned and offered him a paper cup of coffee. "Thank you, Mistress," he repeated when he tasted the sugar in it.

Theresa just shrugged. "Figured a cultured boy like yourself was used to more than black coffee. I, by the way," she said, pointing at him with one of the fingers wrapped around her own cup, "like mine black out here."

The slave let her comment circle in his mind as he tried to decipher what she meant. She'd said something quite similar the day before when she had picked him up. After finishing the coffee, he mounted up behind her, bending over and locking the chain on his right boot to the cycle without being told.

Theresa chuckled. "So far, Adam, you have potential," she said as she slipped her helmet on.

"Thank you, Mistress," he replied as he put his on as well. He moaned deep in his throat as the engine started humming between his legs. When the biker chuckled again as he placed his arms around her, he just closed his eyes and leaned into her.

"He doesn't need a menu," Theresa told the waitress at the diner they had pulled into around noon. The woman popped her chewing gum and tucked the menu back under her arm as she turned and left the table. "I don't remember. You have any food allergies, Adam?"

"No, Mistress," he whispered as he leaned over the table toward him.

"What?" Theresa asked with a grin as she pulled back from the table.

Adam glanced around the diner once then sat up straight and spoke louder. "No, Mistress." Out of the corner of his eyes he would have sworn he saw a few of the nearer patrons glance his way as though they overheard.

The biker, however, leaned forward and motioned for him to do the same. When her hand was wrapped in his bangs she demanded, "Are you ashamed to be mine?"

"No, Mistress, not ashamed," he whispered back. "I thought you might want more discretion in public."

Her hand moved to the collar of his leather jacket as one hands touched her on. "Discretion? With these jackets on?" she teased.

Adam just sat back silently as she released him and picked up the menu. Back at the college, his young master had prized discretion; titles were used only in private or with lowered voices; collars and special clothing were replaced with a simple silver chain around his neck when in public. Likewise, at the estate the slaves behaved just like the free servants when non-House folks were around. The biker seemed completely the opposite of his former masters in her need to let people know of his status. What did these people around him think?

As though reading his thoughts Theresa asked another question. "Are there any types of food you'd rather get fucked by one of those farmers over there than eat?"

Adam coughed and coughed as the biker simply waited for his reply. After several minutes the slave glanced at the group indicated, then back at his owner, his face hot and red. One look into those calm hazel eyes of hers made him realize she was completely serious. "Liver, spinach, cabbage," he said slowly. At her cocked eyebrows he clarified, "I've rather be fucked by those gentlemen than eat those, Mistress."

"Good," the biker replied, then added with a grin, "I hate those things too."

"Ready to order?" the waitress asked as she took her pen from behind one ear.

"Yes, we are," Theresa agreed, then ordered for them both.

An hour later they finished a full lunch, topped off with one sundae, which the biker fed to her property to a few murmurs of "how cute" around them. Only they knew that one of her boots was pressed up against his groin, so his cock was forced to rub into it as he leaned forward across the table for each bite.

When the last bite of ice cream was in his mouth Adam sank back into his chair. To the ice cream he added the remaining ice from his water, hoping the chill would make his erection melt.

The biker took her foot down and signaled for the check. Before it came she got up and headed toward the restrooms, leaving her secretary with money to pay it. The waitress finally smiled after the biker left. "So," she began, an odd twinkle in her eyes, "you're the newest one, huh?"

Adam just stared as he followed the waitress to the cash register and paid the bill. "Thanks, but I think the rest is supposed to be your tip," he said, rejecting the change.

The waitress sighed and slipped the money into her pocket.

"Ready?" the biker asked as she walked out of the women's room and to the front door. "Time to get that hair cut properly," she commented, tossing him a mint that she grabbed on her way out.

"Yes, Mistress," Adam replied before popping the tiny candy into his mouth. He caught the helmet with one hand this time and earned a satisfied smile. Grinning, he put it on and mounted up behind her on the cycle.

The biker led the way into the tiny local barbershop and exchanged grins and nods with the small crowd of men gathered there.

"Hey, Theresa!" the barber called out first, to be echoed by the other men.

"Busy?" the biker asked, pulling her property forward by the arm.

"We can all wait," one of the three men sitting watching the haircuts replied, earning a nudge in his ribs from his companions.

"Ah, Rufus, you old dog. Bet you waited until the grapevine here buzzed that I was back, huh?" Theresa guessed when she walked to the now empty chair as the customer just finished hopped up and handed the barber a bill. "Looks good, Will," she commented as she sat down in the vacated chair.

The newly trimmed man put his glasses back on with a blush.

The barber tilted his head so his ear was near the biker's mouth, but she didn't whisper. "What do you think of him, Donald?"

The barber nodded as he chewed his gum and walked around the slave several times. "A fine piece of work. A fine, fine boy."

"Wish I had money to get me one of those," another customer replied.

"Not me," Rufus said quickly. "I'd get me a girl."

"Yeah, like Ruthy would let you get a girl," the previous speaker teased.

"Fred, you don't know nothing," Rufus responded. "In my home I'm the king."

"Yeah, but Ruthy is the empress," Donald added softly, earning a blush from the teased man and a chuckle from the rest.

Theresa stood up and motioned for her property to take her place. "Jacket," she said holding out her hand.

Adam felt all eyes on him as the jacket slipped off his shoulders, exposing his bare upper body. He was tanned a bit, but not at all like the men were, probably from farm work every day. Out of nowhere a cool draft hit him, causing his nipples to stiffen.

"Very fine," one of the unnamed men replied.

"Adam," Theresa addressed him, "you'll do what these nice men tell you while I'm out. Understand?"

"Yes, Mistress," the slave replied with a quick glance around him.

As the biker turned to go the man called Rufus asked, "Hey what's his, you know, safeword?" The slave blinked first at the fact the country bumpkin would know some terminology. Then again if these men really knew what was going on they wouldn't ask such a question. He'd never had one with the young master though he'd read about them in books and magazines.

"Thought you didn't do boys?" Theresa pointed out with a grin as she paused and looked back. When there was no answer she just sighed and supplied the information to them all. "My name. If he says Theresa, then you stop what you're doing to him."

Adam watched uneasily as the biker walked out of the barber shop and hopped onto her bike again. In less than a minute she was out of sight and he was left with five strange men.

"Sit down," the barber ordered as he flipped the sheet out. "There you go; we'll get your haircut out of the way first," he added as he placed the sheet around the slave's neck.

The actual haircut only took ten minutes, but each cut felt like it was ripping away his memories. Three years had passed since his last haircut, three years since the young master got a job and an apartment, taking his property with him. Adam had been his whore, his secretary, his maid, his anything. And the young master had become his world, a world that was now falling on the floor at his feet, it seemed.

The image in the mirror the barber held before his eyes hardly seemed like himself. The hair was now short and spiky, its black color even darker. His face looked so big and square that Adam had to sniff back a few tears.

"You look fine," the barber said as he took the mirror away. "Now we see how you perform," he added as he lowered the chair.

Adam swallowed as the sheet was removed from his neck. He stood up on command and lifted his hands above his head as the men started circling him, touching his body every now and then. He slipped out of his boots and jeans at their word, and immediately they stepped back to regard him.

"Get the door and windows, Rufus," the barber ordered. The other men stood between the slave and the entrance as the "closed" sign was turned, the door locked and the blinds pulled down. "Now we can have some privacy," the barber said.

Adam watched as the chair's cushions were removed to expose the frame. The metal was smooth as he climbed back into the chair. He noted that the seat now had a big opening in the center which let his ass would hang out. A slight jump was all he could manage as cuffs were placed on both wrists and ankles by four of the men.

"Very nice and smooth," one of the men commented as he ran a hand over the slave's chest. "That's how I like 'em, like a kid," he continued as his hands went down to the nude cock and balls.

"I get him first," the barber said as he tilted the chair's head down. He adjusted the neck brace until the slave's head was supported at the right angle for his cock to penetrate. "Take it in, slave. Show me how much you like a piece of country cock."

Adam swallowed and ran his tongue over his lips quickly, working up moisture before the fat tip was presented to him. As he opened up his mouth and felt it his mind registered that his legs were being parted and raised to his chest. His tongue and mouth worked as trained as hands wandered over his ass. With each playful slap he pressed his lips to his teeth to keep from grazing the barber's cock.

A moan escaped his throat, though, as he felt jelly being pushed into his asshole and then replaced by a cock. The men worked quickly but not roughly, each one taking a turn at his mouth and ass at least once. They teased him, caressing his own hungry cock and lightly slapping his balls. One even licked at his nipples and made him hiss as the flesh was nibbled. As cocks went these five were not bad, though none could be called great. Adam had always thought that farmers would have smelly, dirty rods, but it was clear that these men had prepared for the afternoon. At some level of consciousness he found himself disappointed by that. The young master had often threatened or promised to deliver him to such men when they were on a trip but had never done so.

"Please," Adam begged as he found himself left empty and alone after what he figured was at least three orgasms from each man. His throat was slick and salty; his ass hurt slightly, but the ache of not being filled hurt more. "Please, sirs," Adam begged again.

The men laughed as they unbuckled the cuffs and helped him to his feet. "You liked that, huh?" one of them asked. They laughed as the slave nodded and opened his mouth. "You tired us out, boy," another man answered as he zipped up his jeans.

"Yes, we need some time to recharge," the barber agreed. He reached into one of his pockets and pulled out a chain with two tiny nipple clamps on the Y-shaped end. "You gotta entertain us until we're ready for another go, slave."

"Yes, sir," Adam replied, sticking out his chest to make the nipples more accessible. He sucked in his breath as the clamps bit into the nubs and were tightened. The barber led him into a back room where the other men didn't follow. Adam knelt down between the man's legs and looked up at the offered cock again. From this angle it seemed proper, even religious, to be on his knees taking the limp organ into his mouth.

"Now just work it slow," the barber said with a tiny yank on the chain. "Just enjoy it. Pretend I'm a sultan from one of them there Arab countries that you got to impress." The barber closed his eyes, contemplating his own words, and soon the spent cock swelled into life. After only a few minutes the barber came and grunted as the slave's throat swallowed his cum. "I'll send another of the boys back," the barber said as he released the chain.

Adam groaned as the weight on the nipples pulled sharply. He watched the curtain that separated this room from the main barbershop, and soon the man called Rufus entered. Adam caught the red panties in one hand.

"Put 'em on. You're going to be my girl," Rufus said, his face red and his eyes darting around the room.

Adam looked at the panties and understood how he was supposed to wear them for this fantasy. The open part was on his ass; the front would tightly confine his cock and balls. "How do you want me, sir?"

Rufus scratched his head and motioned towards himself as he went to a cot in one corner of the room. He slid down his pants and exposed the largest of all five country cocks in the shop. Lying down, he stroked himself a few times and then motioned for the slave to mount him. "You can work this now, my girl. Let me feel your hungry cunt milk me dry."

Adam nodded as he mounted, his asshole still damp from the previous use. As he straddled Rufus' groin and worked his ass muscles as his nipples were pinched and pulled by the farmer and the man called him sweet words one might say to a girlfriend such as "Baby doll" and "Pretty little thing." The slave cried out as the man came, giving his nipples one terrible tug as he did so.

The last four men mostly just wanted to play with the nipple clamps or had him suck them off another time. When the last one was getting ready to leave he unscrewed the clamps and removed them; the pain from the blood rushing back made Adam double over.

"Get cleaned up," the barber ordered as he tossed his clothes back to him. Adam stood up, his body shaky. He went into the attached bathroom, took a quick shower, even gargled with some mouthwash. When his ass and throat finally felt more like they had before the orgy, he reentered the shop. The biker was there, sitting on the counter with the register. She patted his head as he knelt at her feet.

"These gentlemen tell me that you entertained them real well," Theresa said. "I have a gift for you," she added, taking his short hair into her fist and lifting up his head. She pointed to a package on one of the waiting chairs.

Adam crawled to it and opened the lid. Inside was a pair of jeans, brand new, along with socks and even a black t-shirt. His jacket and boots were sitting on the chair next to the package. "Thank you, Mistress," he said as he lifted the items out and examined them further.

"Put them on; we need to get going," Theresa announced as she hopped off the counter. She didn't even glance back as she paid the barber against his firm refusal. "Now, you know that you all were doing me a favor," she insisted.

The boots came off quickly and the new jeans slid onto his legs, the stiffness of the fabric nicely pressing into his own slight erection, making it swell a bit. The socks and boots were next, but he saved the T-shirt until last. Adam moved his shoulders and chest a bit causing his to nipples protest at being rubbed against the rougher material and made him close his eyes in pleasure.

"Come on!" the biker called from the open door.

The slave stuffed the older clothing under his arm and swung into his jacket. "Thank you, sirs," Adam said with a quick bow before heading after the biker. As he put his arms around her waist he leaned down to her shoulder. "Thank you, Mistress," he whispered.

Theresa smiled as she drove down the street. "You'll be expected to repay me a thousand times over," she warned.

The bark was rough against his body; some of it crumbled away beneath his fingernails, but he held on as he was pushed against it over and over in a steady rhythm. The silicone cock ramming his ass of course needed no release, so as near as Adam could guess an hour or more had passed since they'd stopped in this wooded area about a quarter of a mile from the road.

"You liked having all those cocks in you, didn't you?" Theresa demanded as she rested against his sweaty shoulder. Fucking was hard work, especially when your own pleasure was as indirect as hers was now.

Adam moaned as he pressed his cheek to the bark. "Yes, oh, yes, Mistress. I'm just a slut. I need you to control me. Please." The correct words had occurred to him fairly soon in this game but she never tired of hearing them.

"What are you?" Theresa asked again as she pulled out and touched him only with her hands on his shoulders.

The feeling was exquisite as he begged and pleaded with words his former owners would have been appalled to hear. "A fuck toy, a hole desperately needing to be filled, a slave to lust." Adam paused for just moment before adding something new. "Your object, anything you want this object to be. Please, please, please, fuck me until I scream!"

Theresa blinked a bit, surprised by what she heard. Under the strap-on she was flooding her own jeans. She removed her hands from his shoulders and a cry like an animal's begging for a beating to stop rose from her slave. With a smile wider than any she'd had in months, she removed the silicone from the harness and knelt to replace it into her saddle backs at her feet.

"Mistress, Mistress, please fuck me, please," Adam was now openly weeping as he begged. No physical restraints held him against the tree but perhaps if he stayed there long enough she'd pity him. His cock pressed against the bark, twitching as though trying to pleasure itself, but he stayed perfectly still with his voice only pleading.

"You still need filling?" Theresa asked as she adjusted the larger dildo in the harness.

"Yes, yes, yes," Adam just repeated over and over. The words became a gasp as something far larger than he'd been taking entered him. Slowly it was pushed in, the length incredible but the width amazing to both his body and his mind. It must have been hidden very well, or else she'd just purchased it back at the small town, for he'd had no idea this was in her bag of tricks. He groaned, biting his arm as her thighs met his asscheeks.

"You don't get to hurt yourself," Theresa scolded as she pulled his head back. With shorter hair it hurt far more than he had been used to. "Do you remember when you wanted me to stop this rape?"

Adam nodded his head as best he could.

"Repeat it, slave," the biker ordered, jerking his head again as she pushed his lower half closer to the tree.

"Until I scream, Mistress. Please fuck me until I scream," he repeated as a tear fell from one eye.

"It better be worth it," Theresa said as she released his head and reached down to the silicone balls between her thighs.

It took a second for the feeling to travel up his ass to his mind and another second for him to register the feeling as sharp jabs of pain-pleasure vibrated into him from the pole within him. Another second passed before his opened mouth released a tree-shaking scream that lasted for minutes as he shot into the bark.

The water was getting cold, but Adam only sat in the tub looking at the bruises on his body from the tree and his fucking, a contented if not confused smile on his lips.

After his rough but mind-blowingly wonderful rape, the biker had helped him into his clothes and back onto her cycle. They had driven for a while then stopped late at this fairly nice hotel right next to the highway. The room had a huge bathtub, and the biker had had him undress as she ran him a bath then helped him in once he was naked.

"How are you doing?" Theresa asked as she peeked in again.

Adam's smile grew into a shy grin as he looked up at her, then down at himself. He blushed as the biker chuckled and came to crouch beside him and test the water with her hand.

"Time to get out; it's getting cold, slave," she announced as she pulled the plug. When he thanked her she just shrugged and walked out.

Adam used the handicapped bars to help himself out onto the towel on the floor. The bruises brought happy sighs to his lips as he dried off his body but once he brought the towel to his short hair that earlier twinge of sadness had returned. Quickly he put everything away.

This was a sub fag's dream, he realized as he paused in the doorway to watch the biker relaxing in one of the chairs in front of the television. Minus the cold leather master, of course. His young master had gotten him to talk about his fantasies and found him books and magazines that described them; he had even promised such nights but never followed through. Thinking back now he remembered that the last time the young master had found him with one of those well-worn magazines he'd ripped it from his hands. That had been just days before being delivered to the Auction House warehouse.

Theresa turned toward him now with a calm look on her face as she motioned him toward her. When he was kneeling by her, that light she'd hoped for shining from his eyes, she spoke. "We'll be home morning after tomorrow. So we'll be riding hard to the hotel I've got a room waiting at. No more rough stuff tonight."

Adam forced himself to smile. "As you wish, Mistress."

"Oh, the pizza will be here shortly," she added, handing him the twenty. "Double-tip this one, he'll be expecting it."

She must have called moments before checking on him in the tub, because he had only a few minutes to consider her words before the knock came on the door. Naked, he went to the door and let the delivery man in this time. He stepped back as the large black man smiled and handed him the pizza, taking the twenty from his hands.

Adam froze as he heard the door lock then set the box on the table. The black man whirled him around and pushed him to his knees. The hard dark cock glistened with precum already as the delivery man and Theresa exchanged a few words. "He is sweet looking," he agreed, then pushed the slave's mouth onto his cock.

Theresa got up and took the pizza box from the table, then went and got the two soft drinks she'd gotten from the machine a bit earlier. Not once did she take her eyes off of the two men as her boy was fucked again. Rough stuff, of course, was only limited to her, not others. The biker smiled when Adam opened his eyes and rolled them toward her. Yes, he did seem to be grinning again as he wrapped his arms around the delivery man's strong marble thighs and pulled himself closer.

Later, at her feet, finishing the last slice, Adam glanced up and wondered why she'd never used him as the men had done. Oh, sure, she'd raped him and made such demands on him with others that even now he could feel a blush rise. But just because his master had been a man didn't mean he couldn't pleasure a woman. Pure homosexuality or heterosexuality was not allowed in any Auction House slave. He swallowed the last bite and was about to ask when she stood up and tossed one of the pillows onto the floor.

"Good night, slave; it will be an early morning," the biker said as she hopped into the bathroom to take her own shower. Later, when she crawled into her own bed she knew that he was still lying there awake, his head spinning with questions, and she just repeated her order to sleep before doing so herself.

The hotel, or rather, motel, was the worst they had stayed in so far. Theresa had double-locked her cycle to the column right in front of the door on the ground floor. She leaned against that same column and looked north across the water toward the lights of the city.

"Mistress?" Adam half yawned as he spoke. The saddle bags were safely in the room and since she had the key, he shut the door behind him and joined her looking at the lights. "New York City," he said, his voice having a half dreamy quality.

"Yes, the Big Rotten Apple or the Big Shiny Apple, depending on where you live," Theresa replied.

The slave nodded silently, considering asking if they'd be living in Alphabet City or Greenwich Village or maybe even Harlem. Probably the second – close to the clubs and sex shops, close to people who thought they lived the same way. "I've been there once, Mistress," he ventured to state and shook his head to fight off another yawn.

"For a visit?"

"Yes, Mistress, about two years ago." That trip had held the most promise; he'd even been placed up for sale in one of the dirty tiny dark clubs. But that had been nothing compared to the feelings he'd experienced back in Florida in the warehouse. It was nothing compared to his new life so far.

"I don't go to the S/M clubs very much," Theresa just stated as she turned and opened the door. "It's after midnight. Time to sleep. We'll shower once we're home."

Adam mumbled his understanding and simply went to brush his teeth and wash his face so she could change into her pajamas alone. When he emerged she squeezed past him, sending charges of frustration through him as their bodies touched briefly.

The less inviting of the two pillows was tossed on the floor, the cover beside it, by the time the biker returned, but the slave was kneeling by her bed. "What's the problem, Adam?" Theresa asked as she jumped over him into the bed.

The slave turned on his knees to face her but kept his face lowered. "Mistress, you have not yet sampled all of my skills," he reminded her, hoping he would not be slapped but needing to risk that as his cock grew just from the vague thoughts running through his mind.

"Oh, you'll be making supper tomorrow night," Theresa chuckled and when his face went an angry shade she poked him with a foot. "I know what you're asking, you slut. I don't do that out here. That's for home. Now go to sleep."

"Yes, Mistress. I'm sorry if I offended you," he offered as he waited.

"Sleep!" Theresa said as she flipped off the light.

Adam crawled to the end of the bed and pulled the cover around him. His whole body ached from the fuckings, the rape, the bike. But the mystery that lay beneath the bed sheets made him ache far worse. The young master and the master had never allowed him to be untouched by them for more than a two-day period, even if only for a five minute suck and a tousle of his hair.

"Oh," Adam groaned. He curled himself into a tight ball and gripped the cover in his fists to keep his hands from himself. Tomorrow he'd see his new home – a tiny space, he was certain, but clean and organized just like the biker herself. Things would settle down a bit more once he was sleeping at the end of her real bed every night.

Adam stood in the main entryway to the highrise holding onto the saddle bags tightly. He watched in a daze as the biker, dressed still in worn jeans, leather boots and bold jacket, spoke at ease with the doorman at this obviously expensive apartment building, or perhaps even condominium, on what he was certain was Park Avenue. At least that was what the sign going north-south had said right before they had pulled into the underground parking garage. The exit had led into the street again right next to the canopy before the front door.

Now the biker and the green-jacketed attendant were chatting in friendly terms. She must work here on the maintenance crew, or maybe she was a doorman as well? Adam heard his name a few times before joining her finally.

"I think he's in shock, Franklin," Theresa said as she clapped one hand around the back of her slave's neck.

"I'd be in shock too, Miss Donnerstein, if you brought me home to a place like this," the doorman replied. He looked up and down the far younger man's body with admiration or perhaps even jealousy. Then another richly dressed woman approached from the elevators, giving the biker and her boy a frown. "I'll hail that cab for you, Mrs. Brownstone," the doorman said with a polite nod to the biker.

"Come on, Adam. Time you got to see where'll you'll be living, for as long as you please me," Theresa added as she led the way to the elevator.

Instead of turning to a side hallway as he expected they entered the elevator. The biker took a set of keys on a plain ring from her inner jacket pocket and placed this into one of the keyholes under the buttons. Then the elevator rose upward and Adam looked at her quickly.

Up they rode until the passed the highest numbered floor and stopped on one marked PH 2. When the elevator stopped, the biker removed the access key, pushed back the safety gate, then unlocked the door in front of them, revealing a fairly fancy hallway.

After following her for a few feet Adam realized that this was the penthouse itself as he found himself in a vast living room with plush carpet and Queen Anne-style furnishings. Over to one side was a door and opposite it a spiral staircase. The slave turned around as he followed her up those stairs and saw a wide-open entryway to a small but elegant dining room and a nearby gourmet-style kitchen at first glance.

At the top of the stairs there was an open door followed by a hallway with another door at the end. "That's my office, at least my home office," Theresa said, pointing to the far door. "This," she said as she opened the door in front of her to reveal an elegant room decorated in red and black silks and oriental rugs, "is my bedroom. Yours, and a bathroom for you, is downstairs, the door opposite these stairs."

Adam just stood still, his mind reeling, every image of her home he'd created shattered when presented with the extremely different reality. He looked up when she took her saddle bag from his hands.

"Take yours downstairs and hit the showers. There's a folder laid out on the bed for you that will tell you all you need to know. Take your time; I'll be a while myself," Theresa said as she took him by the arm and pushed him out the door.

Adam looked at the stairs below him, then back at the closed door. After several deep breaths, he descended and went to the door he'd been instructed to find, being careful to take big steps so as not to dirty the fine carpet more than necessary.

His own room surprised him no less than the rest of the place. It was about the size of half his young master's last residence before he had returned to the manor. The bed was a single, but with a frame, not just a mattress on the floor. There was a small desk, a soft office chair and a regular computer, the same brand as the one he'd been keeping her records up to date on. Two bookcases rose to the ceiling, and the nearby step-stool, he suspected, would allow him access to the top shelves. A glance at the shelves told him that the books were divided into fiction and non-fiction. The non-fiction had titles such as "How to Entertain Large Groups," "A Thousand Holiday Ideas," and various grammar and etiquette books. The fiction had the classics of English literature, and he realized with a shock that several of the books were the ones he himself had had.

He dropped the saddle bag on the floor – hardwood, well-kept – and took several of the familiar books. He stepped back and looked out the door toward the stairway. These were his books, with his name and the dates he'd purchased them inside the covers.

Adam slipped out of his jacket and tossed it onto the bed as he picked up the folder laying there. It was a guidebook to how Theresa expected him to behave, describing her rules and her regular schedule in clear language. He quickly glanced through it with a bemused smile on his face. This was not at all what he'd been expecting when she bought him, and yet it was very near to what he had expected growing up on the estate of his former owners. An itch on his scalp reminded him that he needed a shower.

The shower, too, had all the necessary supplies; it had even been noted that he didn't need face-shaving supplies and that he needed sensitive-skin and fragrance-free products to accommodate his allergies. The shower was large, and he was glad to be able to lean back against a clean wall and let the steam and hot water surround him. He made sure he was completely clean inside and out before turning off the water, turning on the exhaust fan, and drying off.

Naked, he now looked through the bureaus and found clothing his size, including a few of the sweaters he had received as gifts over the years. The closet also showed the same high quality of clothing, things that his masters had worn, but never he himself. On one end, however, were jeans and T-shirts and a couple of empty hangers. On one he put the leather jacket with the boots under it; the jeans and T-shirt he tossed into the dirty clothes hamper.

Clothes: there were a couple of pages on this in the folder, so he now read through these carefully. He pulled out cotton boxers and casual sandals, then cotton pants and a tunic-style shirt marked with the same code numbers showing what could be worn with what. He reasoned that since she hadn't mentioned a fancy affair he should stick with the casual indoor attire.

A curse from her and the sound of stomping downstairs made him hurry the tunic over his head before leaving his room to stand at the edge of the living room. He blinked as the biker – no, this was not a biker – descended the stairway with a pair of pumps in one hand and holding a cordless phone in the other.

"I just got back, Eric; I have a couple of more days left on my vacation this season, you know," she told the other person on the phone as she stepped into her pumps.

Adam looked at her and realized that it was indeed the biker who'd bought him, or at least the same woman, though clearly in a different role now. She was in a light pink suit jacket with matching knee length shorts with a pair of pearl earrings matching the single thin string around her neck. Her hair was swept up into a bun clipped with a matching pearl comb.

Theresa glanced at her new slave with a tired smile as she listened and nodded at the telephone. "Yes, I'll be there within a half an hour or so. But Eric, you tell Thompson that he owes me big time for this and he loses half his own vacation time if this doesn't deliver as promised." She put one hand over the mouthpiece and asked Adam, "Is your stuff there as well?"

"Yes, Mistress," he managed to reply.

"And you, Eric, have just had one lucky break today, so don't blow it when I get in. Good-bye," she said as she clicked off the phone, then dialed it. "I'll need my car immediately."

Adam followed her to the elevator, where she grabbed the keys she'd laid on a small table with mail piled up in a basket sitting on it and a briefcase of white leather under it. She took the briefcase as well then paused to smile at her new slave.

"I'll call you before I head home for supper. You have the day free; please read the folder. I'll need excellent service tonight," she stated as the elevator doors opened. "Or I might just have to rape you again," she added, the twinkle he'd seen on the journey sparkling briefly in her eyes before she left.

Adam leaned against the elevator doors and listened to it descend. There must be a way to do both. He smiled and went back to collect the folder, certain that the answers would be there, though hidden under rules and regulations, just as the biker herself was now hidden under that linen and perfume. The fantasies suddenly seemed less enticing to him as he realized that not everything was as it seemed – nor should it be.

Justice

"Justice" is the sequel to "Punishment for the Crime," a story in my first published erotica collection with the same title. "Punishment" is the story of Jake Monroe, a convicted drug dealer who has been sentenced to slavery for his crimes. Princess Yvonne, known as "the Butcher" for her military exploits, takes an interest in Jake and conditions him to be loyal only to her and to respond to her sexually. She makes it clear that she could tire of him at any time.

Later, Jake is summoned from the palace to join Yvonne in her tent on the battlefield, where he arouses the jealousy of General Valerie Corriger, Yvonne's right hand and sometimes lover. Corriger tortures Jake nearly to death, but Yvonne saves him just in time. In the end, although Jake is treated for his injuries and allowed to recover, Yvonne leaves his future ominously uncertain.

DRIP. PLOP. DRIP. PLOP. DRIP. PLOP.

He lost count around half a million and found himself falling into a pool of water. As the waves rocked and swirled, climbing his chest, splashing against his chin, Jake screamed. The cry echoed back from the darkness. There was no water around him except for that maddening drip.

The day he had been released from the palace hospital was stuck in his mind. The doctor, a kind woman, had been very quiet, refusing to look at him as he was escorted from the room he had shared with other injured royal slaves into a back office. She had neither spoken to him nor looked at him as she had instructed her assistants on what to do.

At first it had seemed like he was being prepared for a meeting with his owner. He had been shaved, given an enema, his vitals signs checked, and even given a nasty health drink. He had been dressed in loose, easily removable clothing and escorted out of the hospital. The doctor had touched his arm briefly but hadn't spoken; she had just looked at him with her sad brown eyes.

He had been taken into a completely dark room and restrained with ankle and wrist cuffs. His legs and arms had been pulled until he cried out.

His clothing had been removed. He had known better than to speak or to cry out when the beating began.

The method of beating had concerned him only in that it had been unusual for Yvonne. She liked to switch from one whip to another, intersperse the beating with threats in his ear, taking breaks for food and drink. This beating, however, had begun hard, with a leather cat of at least nine tails, each with knots at the end. The blows had come in a steady rhythm, also unlike his owner's style.

The beating had paused and he had heard a second pair of footsteps in the room. With a nervous swallow Jake had ventured to ask his question. "Mistress, why are you doing this?" There had been silence, and then the rain of blows had fallen again. The beating had continued until the lightning sting of the lashes simply disappeared. He suspected he had fallen unconscious, but no one had answered him when he demanded to know what was going on.

At first he had tried to count the days as they passed in total darkness. He had based his count on the assumption of one meal per day, which he had figured was all this punishment would allow. It had to be a punishment; the alternative was unthinkable, impossible.

Those first few days he had asked the unseen owner of the hands that fed him what he had done wrong. Pressing the question over and over had confirmed a fear. His mistress was not the one feeding him, for she would have hit him, or at least reminded him firmly that only one question was allowed each day. So he had then asked who he had been given to, since there was no reported crime that he was here for. That question had only been met with laughter, laughter far away, perhaps three yards, and yet clearly the Princess Yvonne's voice.

Jake now bit his cheek. The shackles on his hands, stretched out to his sides, made it impossible to plug his ears. So now he tried to hurt himself in any way he could to pull his mind away from the sound and the answer he was searching for but which alluded him. The royal family never sold slaves. Yvonne had told him she wouldn't give him away. That left one alternative only, and it was too horrible to think of.

The water stopped just as he burst into tears moments later. And Jake then quieted himself and listened carefully. No, there was not even a tiny remnant of the sound. He swung his head back into the air. Except for his feet on the cold stone floor and the metal on his ankles and wrists he wasn't in contact with anything other than the air.

The hair on the back of his neck rose as he heard footsteps approaching. This would be food, at least, and a chance to try and get answers. He jerked back when something touched his face, tickling the beard that was growing now after at least two weeks by his feeble calculations. Her laughter hit his ears. "Mistress, please," he muttered as he reached out with his dry tongue, trying to touch her.

"Ah, still trying to please me?" Yvonne asked.

"Yes, Mistress, Jake is trying to please you. Please tell your slave what to do?" he begged and choked slightly on a cry in his throat.

"You enjoy pleasing me, don't you, Jake?"

Jake opened his eyes and could barely make out a human figure against the darkness. "Yes, Mistress. It is your slave's existence."

"But you enjoy it a great deal. Correct?" Yvonne's voice had a dangerous edge to it.

"Yes, Mistress," Jake simply replied. He licked his lips as she laughed again.

"And that is the problem," Yvonne began. "You see, drug dealer, you're supposed to be punished, not having a holiday. I guess enslavement just isn't appropriate for you."

Jake's mouth fell open as he heard the words and the thoughts in his head, the ones he had until now so successfully ignored He called after the retreating footsteps, "Mistress! Please, Mistress! Please, come back! Please!" His crying died down as he heard the door shut.

There was no food after this. No water dripping either. Nothing to help him count the time. Just the torment in knowing she was starving him to death.

Try as he might, he just couldn't accept it; it just made no sense. The princess was cruel but fair. Yvonne was strong but beautiful. He had been blessed with her smile on a few occasions. She had even fired her lover in his defense. She cared for him; he had been so certain.

In later moments he would remember that she was called the Butcher for a reason. After that moment he gave up hope of even seeing the world beyond the dungeon. Weeping, spending the last energy he had, he prayed that God, whatever that was, would forgive him.

Jake blinked his eyes as best he could as he vaguely felt his body being lifted. His arms and legs were numb, and yet he knew they had been uncuffed. His head throbbed loudly as it swung. A look into the darkness showed the dungeon upside down as he was moved.

"Fuck! He's still not light." A hauntingly familiar voice reached through his pain and hunger.

"What's ... going ... on," he whispered as the dungeon receded. A door was shut behind him, and the light outside was brighter. From his position over the shoulder of this new tormentor he could see military-style boots. Perhaps he had assumed too quickly that death would come easily in the confines of the dank prison.

A scent was the first signal Jake's brain registered. It was a warm, soft scent like flowers in the woods under the sunlight after a gentle rain. "Thank you," he whispered to God.

"You're welcome," a woman's voice answered.

Jake opened his eyes slowly and focused on the voice's owner, a woman of thin build with long brown hair wrapped into several locks by ribbons. Dressed in brown shorts and a tank top she hardly represented the angel he'd been expecting. His attempt to sit up met with little success, so he sighed and just watched as his caretaker pulled up a chair and sat next to him. "Who are you?" he asked.

"Ann," the woman replied simply. "If you think you can eat something, I'll help you," she added. Her voiced had an unfamiliar accent to it.

Jake nodded slowly, then tried to sit up again. This time the angel helped him by lifting his shoulders and placing a few pillows beneath him. He looked around the room as well as his weakened state allowed. It wasn't anywhere he'd been before and was far too Spartan for the Butcher's tastes. Maybe she'd changed her mind and just given him away.

"Here is some soup with those cute tiny crackers you have," Ann said as she pulled the chair up closer. She held out a spoonful and let him eat at his own pace. "You must start slow," she added when he reached for the bowl himself.

Jake waited to ask the important questions until he had finished the soup, the tray was taken away, and he was lowered back down onto the bed. "So where am I?"

The angel blinked at him with a smile.

"Who owns me now?" he asked but received the same silence. "Look, I'm not going to cause problems; I'd just like to know what's expected of me."

Ann stood up. "To get well again." She moved the chair away and left his view.

In the background he heard a door open, shut and lock. Jake sighed, cursed himself for being in such a situation in the first place, and then cursed God for not answering his prayer.

With the Butcher it had been a punishment but also a pleasure, one ripped from him everyday, forced from his body in delightfully wicked ways. A new owner was just another inconvenience to be endured and fought against. As he yawned and felt sleep take him over, the image of a cruel face framed by shoulder-length blood-red hair filled his sight. "Mistress," he moaned into the darkness.

He spent the next five days resting, eating a increasingly complex diet, and attempting to get answers from the angel. Jake set the half-eaten wheat roll on his tray and looked directly at his nurse. "When are you going to answer my questions?"

Ann just smiled and started to take his tray.

Jake caught her hands in his and sat up so their faces were inches apart. "I want to know where I am and who is having you do all this!"

"My, my, my," a new voice interrupted. It was the same voice that he'd heard when he'd been carried from the dungeon. The sound made him release the angel and look around the room. From a poorly-lit corner a figure emerged. With her blonde hair cut much shorter than it had been during her time as the heir's chief aide, it took the slave a couple of seconds to recognize her. Corriger chuckled when realization flashed in his eyes. "Oh, yes, it's me again. Isn't this a surprise?" she mocked him as she motioned for the angel to leave.

Jake looked at Ann but didn't attempt to speak to her as she removed his lunch tray. He glared at the jealous general as he braced himself for flight if necessary and possible. "You're the last person I want to be owned by," he said flatly.

"And you're the last person I'd ever want to own," Corriger replied. "So you'll be as relieved as I when tell you that I don't own you."

"Then who? Who do you work for now?" Jake's mind filed through the images of big corporate bosses who hired personal security forces and the aristocracy he'd seen in the palace from time to time. It made sense now. Yvonne had been planning to kill him but needed to use him for political gain.

"You'll see soon enough," Corriger replied. She walked to him and looked down at him, her hands at her sides, fists clenched. "Get up!"

Jake's fear melted as the hatred he felt for this woman who had ended his life flared up. "No." The blow was expected, but still it sent him half-falling out of bed. He looked up at her and licked the blood at the corner of his mouth. "The answer is still no," he tossed out with a snort.

"Ann!" Corriger called out, and immediately the angel returned and stood next to her, her beautiful face attentively watching the woman. "Get up, boy!"

Jake shook his head, then gasped as the general grabbed the slave girl by her hair then backhanded his angel of mercy.

"Each time you disobey me, I'll punish your little nurse," Corriger stated. She yanked the slave, for now Jake could recognize the collar around the gentle creature's neck, to her feet. "Get up!"

Jake swallowed once then rose to his feet, his eyes flashing. "Leave her alone," he said, his voice low and as threatening as it could be given his position.

Corriger laughed and then bent the angel's head back and planted a big kiss on her bruised lips. The slave responded by touching the general's arms lightly, embracing her. Corriger released Ann and smiled at Jake as he made a gagging sign with his fingers pointing toward his mouth. "Ann, take him and get him cleaned up, as I explained earlier."

"Yes, Mistress," the slave angel said. She held out her hand to Jake, who took it eagerly.

Once outside the room and into a bathroom several yards down a hall that seemed vaguely familiar in that it was large, like all homes of the rich and spoiled, Jake pushed his companion against the wall gently. "You and me, let's get out of here."

"And go where?" Ann asked with a tiny frown as she pulled free of him.

"Anywhere that isn't here. There must be a country that doesn't have good relationships with the United Lands, Eastland," he added at the slavegirl's frown. "We'll find out who hates this place most and go there," he said. He slammed his fist into the wall as the girl just shook her head. "Look, I've run before, it can be done."

"And you've always been caught," Ann pointed out as she turned to the bathtub.

"Well, I'm a little better educated now. If you can tell me where we are and how far from the border, I can get us there," he promised.

Ann knelt down by the tub as it filled with water. "No. Now get out of those clothes and into the tub. We have a lot of work to do."

Jake sighed and agreed silently by taking off the soft sleep shirt. The truth was that he wasn't ready to run, not until he learned more of what was going on and figured out some way to make the blonde bitch Corriger pay for losing him the best thing he'd had in years. He'd been a slave, but at least it was to royalty, and he'd had more freedom there than he'd ever had in the city he'd been born in. Not that he would ever admit any of this to anyone, not even to the Butcher.

"So what did you do to be enslaved?" Jake asked once he was settled into the tub. He chuckled as the slave girl's soapy sponge tickled his sides.

"Nothing," Ann said. She dipped the sponge deeper, moving it in tight circles as she stroked his cock and thighs. She watched his face, but he only looked back at her, the organ under her hand not changing in the least. Frowning, she pulled one leg up from the water and started working on it.

Jake caught himself on the sides of the tub with his arms. "Hey, take it easy," he said. "So you were sold for a debt then?" he guessed.

"No, just captured by Yvonne the Butcher," the slave girl stated.

Jake sat up and pulled his legs under him. "You're from another country? Damn, I knew you had an accent!" Ann nodded and moved up so she could work on his back. There was silence, then Jake inquired further. "So why haven't you been ransomed yet?"

"Who would ransom a slave? Very easily replaced where I'm from," Ann said with a guffaw.

"I don't understand," Jake said. "What kind of place are you from?"

"Someplace where they don't even pretend to have laws," Ann said, and Jake sensed that there was a bit of sadness in that answer. "A place where you're born into your station in life without hope of change."

"That sounds sucky," Jake sighed. "So I suppose you like Corriger better than what you had before?" he asked.

There was a pause. "Yes. Her demands are of a more personal nature." There was a shy giggle. "I'd always been taught God would strike you with lightning for joining with another of your own sex," she admitted. "But I'm still here, and better fed and clothed than before. It was all a bit confusing."

"But not now?" Jake asked as the angel stood up and pulled a chair to the tub. She nodded and handed him a razor. "Oh, great, I get to see what I look like," he said as she held a mirror up to him. His face was covered with dark brown and black hair, but it wasn't very long, maybe indicating only two to three weeks of growth. "I take it my new owner likes the clean-shaven look?"

"I don't really know. I've never met her," Ann answered.

Jake's eyes glanced at the slave girl then back at the mirror as he tucked this needed information away. Very carefully he shaved and washed his face, his mind whirling with the opportunities that could await him if given half a chance, good food, and a better wardrobe.

Jake walked as stiffly as Corriger's tight grip on his arm allowed. When he had left the bathroom, she had immediately grabbed him and inspected him closely. He had been angry and embarrassed by her prodding and poking, especially when she had insisted he perform an enema on himself. It had taken just one more slap of Ann for him to obey, though he ground his teeth angrily as he did so.

The humiliation had not been merely from the fact that Ann was watching or that the general was forcing him, but from the fact that as the water filled him and then rushed out he found himself hard and aching for any type of touch. He had retaliated by jerking off right onto the general's boots. His thoughts, however, had not been of revenge but of being abused by the cruel princess whose brand still marked his ass.

So now he was being shoved down the hallway, his arm twisted behind his back and up to the opposite shoulder, completely naked, his cheeks still red and burning from the slaps he had earned. A grin curled his lips as he made the march as difficult as he dared.

The general opened the door with one hand and shoved him through so that he landed on his side. The carpeted floor was a light green, the color called Sea Foam in the catalogs his mother used to collect and read before turning them in for a recycling fee. "Stand up, you fucking bastard!" Corriger yelled.

Jake looked around the room slowly without answering. The room was well lit, but no one else seemed to be waiting for them. He cried out between clenched teeth as he was kicked in the ass. "Don't you remember, general? Beating me doesn't work much, at least not for you. Sure you don't want to go get a horse to tie me behind?" he tossed out with a sneer as he refused to look up at her.

"Stand up, or I'll make you wish you were back in that dungeon!" Corriger threatened.

"I already do!" Jake yelled back.

The general readied to kick him again when a voice stopped her and caused the slave to sit up.

"Now, now, general. Is violence the only method you know?" The voice was coming from behind a desk, large and modern looking, a computer sitting on it along with several monitors. The leather-covered chair with a high back was hiding the speaker. "There are so many other ways to get someone do as you wish," the voice continued.

Jake stood up as the chair rotated slowly. He placed his hands in front of his groin, suddenly too aware of his nakedness. This was not how he had planned to make a good impression on his new owner, and first impressions would dictate how easily controlled she could be. The voice didn't sound old, so he just hoped the face would be average and not ugly, though it would hardly matter if he got what he wanted.

"Money, power, love, blackmail," the voice rattled on. "These are all other methods that can be used to elicit the choice you wish the person to make."

The chair stopped, and Jake opened his mouth slightly as he saw the woman. Her features were familiar, and for a moment he was ready to throw himself on the floor and crawl the distance to the boots he loved so well. But the hair was much longer, braided into two plaits and even darker red. The eyes, too, were larger, and the face fuller. The clothing wasn't military at all; it looked like an elegant suit, the coat green and the shirt underneath black to set off the pale skin; both reflected the light as silk might. This was a person who didn't spend her time outdoors on raids or murder runs.

In her hands, the nails far better manicured than the Butcher's had ever been, was a rat. Not one of the white ones folks kept as pets, but one of the mangy ones that plagued the cities and the poor. Its muzzle was taped shut, and the woman patted its trembling head as she spoke, one hand wrapped gently around the body. "But I suppose that Yvonne never used much that wasn't physical. She just can't live in the real world, where we're all forced to deal with one another's decisions, their choices affecting our own."

Jake shuddered as the woman's hands moved quickly and he heard a tiny snap from the rat's now-motionless body.

"With people, though, I agree that violence is sometimes necessary," the woman said. She looked at the dead rat with a sad frown before tossing it to the general, who caught it with a disgusted groan. "Isn't that correct, Jake?" the woman said as she leaned forward, placing her arms onto her desk.

At this distance, it was like looking into the past as a younger Butcher smiled at him. Jake only swallowed, afraid to do anything else for several minutes while the younger Yvonne stared at him. Her eyes were green like the queen's, her nose was regal like the king's, and her voice was deep and steady like Yvonne's.

The woman leaned back with a laugh. She stood up and approached Jake. Now he saw that she was taller than Yvonne had been and wider; she wore black pants and soft-looking black shoes; her hair was in three braids, not the normal two he'd assumed. She looked him directly in the eyes as she dropped the bomb. "I'm Angelique. Yvonne's little sister. Now," she continued speaking as she backed up and motioned to a chair by the desk, "please do sit down."

Jake looked behind him and found himself alone in the room. Months ago he would have tried the door or the window, but something in the eyes told him that Angelique's security would be as thorough as Yvonne's. He sat down then, crossing his legs to hide himself from her view. It seemed like incest somehow to be seen by his Mistress' kid sister.

He waited silently as the second princess regarded him and closed down her computers. The younger princess leaned back in her chair, hands behind her head, and just looked at him. After watching her stare for several minutes, Jake finally spoke. "So, I've been given to you, your majesty?"

Angelique laughed again. "Oh, no. I've had you stolen," she said.

Jake just frowned and watched as she laughed. Part of him wanted to thank her, while the other part wanted to call his real owner's room. After a moment he leaned forward. "Are we still in the palace?"

"Yes, and she can't find you," Angelique said. There was calmness in her face, but a mad joy radiated from her voice. "She's had three people killed since you disappeared five days ago."

"She's looking for me?" he asked, a desperate hope in every fiber of his being.

"Yes," Angelique stated more seriously. "But not because she cares about you. You do realize that, don't you? She was enjoying watching you die, slowly, agonizingly. You do know that?"

Jake slumped back into his chair and nodded. So here he was, kidnapped but perhaps rescued, if she was telling the truth. No sibling had been mentioned by Yvonne, the king or the queen in his hearing. Vaguely he remembered some news clips that had mentioned a younger princess, something about college too, but those images were old in his mind. He sighed and decided to play along. "Yes, I know that, Your Majesty."

"Good. Then you will accept me as your new owner?" Angelique asked. Her green eyes narrowed, and her body poised for action based on his answer.

"I haven't much choice, My Lady," Jake said as he stood up. He placed his hands behind his back as he stood straight.

Angelique also stood. "There are always choices," she stated flatly.

True to her word, Angelique was now standing off to one side watching silently as Jake looked at the three sets of clothes that were lying on her bed. The clothing was very much like that which he'd worn in the camp: soft, rich, the symbol of a slavery steeped in more than mere menial tasks. Jake ran his hands through his hair. Oddly, it had not been cut, so the spiky design he'd grown used to was now slightly wavy. "I get to choose?" he asked with a glance at her.

Angelique nodded. "If you don't like any of them..."

"Oh, no, that's not it," Jake countered quickly. "I'm just wondering which you'd prefer," he stated with a smile meant to charm.

"I like all of them; that's why they're here in the first place," Angelique said as she removed her jacket and tossed it onto the divan sitting by the window.

The tank top she wore showed that underneath, what had at first appeared softer and rounder than the heir's was instead stronger, thicker; her entire body now seemed leaner as well, and it struck Jake as slightly funny. Little Sister wasn't little in any sense of the word. He picked up the middle shirt and focused on it to keep from laughing. He held it up. "Think this tan color will show off my eyes?" he asked with a grin.

"It's taupe," Angelique corrected. "Looks fine. If you wish you may keep the others as well; just hang them up in there," she added as she walked past him and tapped on the door of a wardrobe. "I'll be back in about half an hour," she added as she left the room.

Jake waited until he had heard another door open and close, then bolted to the windows. Both were locked, but no shock sent him flying as had happened in the heir's suite. The two suites were almost identical: office below, with a spiral staircase leading up to the bedroom. The rooms were quite different, though. Black, clearly, was the primary color for both, probably because the national flag was black with a white royal coat of arms on it. But while Yvonne's suite was militant and blood red, this one had greens and browns, and even other colors, in the nature designs on most of the black lacquered furniture.

Jake crossed the wooden floor to the front door and found it locked as well but not electrified as he'd expected. Standing near the door he noticed the first weapons in the room. Two sticks; no, staffs, he corrected himself, as he walked toward them. They were set on pegs in one wall, and underneath were several daggers with richly decorated wooden handles. On a small table under them was a statue of a female being with eight arms who seemed to be regarding him seriously.

Jake shuddered and stepped back. *Just stick around and play this out,* he cautioned himself. He pulled on the clothing – no underwear again, so perhaps that was indeed common slave garb around here. It all fit him well, even the sandals. As he buttoned up the shirt his fingers brushed his metal collar, and he sighed, remembering how used to it he had become. Somewhere in his mind his conscience was telling him to scream and rip it from his throat. His hands, however, didn't know how to do that anymore, and the rest of his mind informed him that there was little point.

His wardrobe had a black bag sitting in the bottom, he discovered when he went to place the other two sets of clothes inside. After hanging things up he pulled it out and set it on the floor. It looked very familiar, the scent of the leather making him quake with memories he had given up when death had seemed around the corner. Inside he found the items which had become far too much a part of his life.

"Are those yours?" Angelique's voice made him look up. She was standing there, her hair combed down around her head and her face still damp, a towel wrapped around her. "Yvonne threw those out a few weeks back when she returned from her last campaign. I thought they might have something to do with you," she added as she flipped the sides of her hair back with a comb and snapped barrettes into place.

"She threw them out?" Jake heard himself ask, then bit his lip as he zipped the bag back up.

"Sure; that is her usual pattern of behavior after she gets rid of a slave," Angelique said.

Jake was silent as she walked out of sight again. *Idiot! You didn't actually think you were special, did you?* he cursed himself as he put the bag back into the wardrobe. He examined the wardrobe closely but found nothing else except a pair of brown silk pajamas and a shaving case in the one drawer at the bottom. Simple but elegant – there was a theme here, he suspected.

Jake was looking at the bed, noting that there were further similarities between Angelique and the heir in the form of cuffs attached to the posts at head and foot. Unlike Yvonne's rough metal, though, these were leather and padded. He ran his hands over one and tried it on his wrist.

"You interested in things like that?" It was Angelique's voice again. This time she was in a green dress that clung to her body, the neckline plunging low to show off ample cleavage. She chuckled as the slave set the cuff down, stood up, and swallowed at her. "Not quite my sister's style, huh?" she said, making a turn.

"No, not at all," Jake said, then looked down while hastening to add, "My Lady."

"You may call me Mistress if you prefer," Angelique offered as she opened a matching handbag and looked inside.

"Is that an order?" he asked, an edge he didn't really mean in his voice.

Angelique grinned. "No, just another choice for you."

"And if I decide to just call you My Lady, what will you do to me or have done to me?" he asked bluntly.

She moved far more quickly that he could have imagined her heels would allow and was standing directly in front of him. "Nothing," Angelique said as she touched his shoulders with her hands. He flinched at the contact, and she clicked her tongue. "My actions are based on yours; nothing will happen to you here that you don't ask for one way or another," she explained.

Jake blinked, then set his mouth as his old dislike of those with more than himself surfaced. "What's to keep me from walking out of here or hurting you?"

The grin broke into a chuckle as Angelique slid her hand down one of his arms. "Why, your promise to obey me as your owner," she said. Suddenly she moved, and Jake found himself slammed face down onto her bed, his arm twisted violently behind his back. "Unless you're confirming the stereotype that a drug dealer's word is nothing but a pack of lies?" she challenged lightly as she pushed up on his arm, causing him to cry out.

Jake took a deep breath as he tried to figure out what had just happened. As his arm was twisted more he answered, "No, I will obey you, My Lady." He lay there as she released his arm and the bed moved. When she touched his cheek, he pulled back but just far enough to watch her as she sat down next to where he lay. She sat so calmly, one leg crossed over the other at the knee so the slit in her dress went up to her thigh at least, that serene look on her face betrayed only by the gleam in her eyes. "Unless your sister finds me and reclaims me, I am your slave now," he added.

The green eyes rolled up toward the ceiling as though considering the possibilities in his words. Then Angelique stood up and walked to the main door. She turned after opening it. "I'll bring you back something to eat. Please feel free to look around and make yourself at home, Jake."

What the fuck? Jake lay flat on the bed, breathing slowly and moving his arm slightly. It hurt, but at least it moved, so it wasn't broken. As he relaxed he noticed that the canopy overhead continued the nature theme. There above him was a stream set near grove of trees, with deer and other animals drinking while a group of women watched from their position deeper in the woods. Behind them there was a deer roasting on a spit over a fire while one woman, her hair reddish and in braids, looked blissfully at the flames. He sat up and looked more closely at that woman with red hair; her fingers were at her lips. "Ugh," he said as he realized she was tasting the blood on her hand.

"This is more scary than my mistress' room," he told the empty room as he stood up. "What would she do if I found her, let her know where I was, offered myself to her?" he asked himself as he looked out the locked window. A lump of ice-cold fear formed in the pit of his stomach, making him shiver. He looked at the staircase, then headed for it and the office below.

The royal dinner table was quiet until the last dish had been set on the table and the servants and slaves dismissed by the queen. The daughter in dress military uniform leaned across the table. "What are you doing back here?" she asked, sounding both angry and surprised. "I thought you were off on some diplomatic mission bullshit."

"Yvonne, please!" the queen said, her genteel face blushing deeply.

As the heir was about to speak, the king slammed his fist down on the table, making all three pairs of female eyes swing toward him. "Enough! You two act as though you were still children, which you are not!"

"Forgive me, father," Yvonne said with an incline of her head. "I'm simply surprised by Angelique's presence. I'm normally informed of all guests at the palace," she added with a glare toward the king.

"You were informed of this as well, but you've been paying little attention to things outside your own private dungeon," the king replied, breaking off to cough several times, causing the queen to rise from her seat and hurry toward him. "I'm fine; stop hovering," he said with difficulty. The women were silent as the queen returned to her seat, the youngest daughter reaching over the table and taking her mother's hand.

"It sounds worse," Yvonne commented slowly.

"Yes," the king stated. He held up his hand so that no one interrupted him. "Now I need to have a meeting with the both of you. Angelique has done very well in the West and across the seas in that direction. You need to be informed of this, Yvonne. She is to be your chief advisor and will have a place on the counsel," he reminded them all.

Yvonne frowned and muttered something under her breath.

"It is my wish, so it shall be done!" the king ordered.

"Don't worry, sister," Angelique said with a warm smile. "You are the heir."

"Who you'd like to see removed for your own benefit," Yvonne snarled. The calm she held like a dagger over everyone's head had vanished in the past five days. The appearance of the one person she truly detested here certainly didn't help. "But you're not strong enough to rule, and you know it," the heir added with a sneer as she sat back in her chair.

"Stop it!" the king bellowed, which set off another fit of coughing. He picked up his napkin, and when he removed it from his mouth the queen gasped and stood up. The king shook his head as his youngest daughter's eyes widened at the sight of the blood. "You see now why I recalled you," he said as he swallowed and winced at the pain in his chest.

"Yes, father," Angelique said softly. "You will have no problems with me as long as Yvonne chooses to treat me with sisterly respect," she added with a direct look into the dark eyes opposite hers. "I merely wish to do my duty to parents, king, and state."

Yvonne rolled her eyes and turned to her food. Out of the corner of her eye she watched her father's slowed movements. The ring which marked her as heir seemed to itch a bit as she considered the near future. Her mind, however, was cursing the fact that this meeting about trade and peace would keep her from her scheduled questioning in the dungeon. She narrowed her eyes at her sister as the kid smiled and laughed at the story their mother told her about her latest foolish shopping trip. The Butcher was surrounded by fools, dying old men, and thieves. Deal first with one, and then the others.

Jake tapped his finger against each book as he read the titles silently. A search of both the office and the bedroom suite confirmed that the layout was much the same as the other princess', right down to the electronic devices for pulleys and so forth around the bed itself. The servants' entrance was locked and the telephones disconnected. No fancy electrical shocks, no guards waiting outside on the balcony, just simple locks. He was still a slave; this one was just more subtle about it.

Most of the books looked academic, boring and beyond his understanding or interest. Some words he recognized like "history," "philosophy," and "science," but there were other words he didn't really understand, though he could read them. The books lined two of the four walls completely as far as the needed doors, stairway, and window allowed. It was like one of those old libraries they sometimes showed on television, the ones only the rich had or the fairly well-off could afford cards to.

Her desk was unlocked, and that surprised him greatly. He'd have been beaten within an inch of his life for even looking into the desks of any of the others who'd owned him; Yvonne would have just killed him outright. *That's what I should have done then*, he decided with a disappointed sigh. The desk contents weren't interesting at first glance. Normal desk things, his knowledge once more based on television shows he had seen, like pens, pencils, paper, disks for the computer, scissors. Then a few more intriguing items like an address book with places he knew to be incredibly far away and others he'd never even heard of. There was even a mini refrigerator to one side about the size of a six pack.

In the bottom drawer of the desk, right underneath the computer keyboard arm, were three large books. When he removed them his sight fell on images of several men, all handsome, all almost entirely nude, and all restrained by various means, the chief of which were webs made of rope. The books had no titles, only dates on their covers, and when he opened them he found more pictures, identified by names and dates. There was no other text, only the captured men, and unlike the picture books Yvonne kept these men all smiled back at him from beneath the protective plastic.

"There you are!"

The voice made Jake bolt and hit his head on the desk so that he rolled out onto his side, clutching at the bump forming there. He released the book he'd been looking at into unfamiliar hands, then accepted their aid in getting him to his feet.

"Didn't mean to scare you quite so much," the voice said. It was masculine so Jake opened his eyes. "Do you feel dizzy?" the man asked.

Jake nodded a bit and let the man sit him down in the window seat. He watched silently as the man knelt and returned the books to their place. This unfamiliar man was about his own size, his hair blond and his skin well tanned. When he looked up at Jake there was an amused twinkle in his blue eyes.

"Let's get back upstairs," the man said as he rose to his feet. He wore simple clothes but had no collar around his neck marking him as a slave. The clothes were not the uniform of the servants in the palace either, so Jake was wary. "Come on, I'll explain a few things once we're back upstairs," the man promised.

Jake silently went up the stairs in front of the other man. He took a deep breath and was about to ask some questions when a hand was pressed against his mouth. A cloth was forced between his lips and teeth and tied tightly behind his head. He grunted as the man pushed him forward onto the bed. If there was one thing Jake feared more than death in the dungeon it was another rape by another man. He braced his legs and struggled as his hands were likewise tied behind him. When he was pushed onto his side he glared at the man and tried to kick at him.

"Calm down," the man said. "Look," he explained as he held up his hands and stepped back, "I don't want to hurt you. I just need you to be quiet for a while."

JUSTICE AND OTHER SHORT EROTIC TALES

Jake grunted, then stopped as he heard the door to the office below open. He heard two sets of footsteps, one the click of high heels and the other the sound of boots. He swallowed as he thought he recognized those boots.

"Please don't make any noise," the man begged him softly as he sat down on top of him, his hand placed over the gag.

The voices were quite clear, and Jake closed his eyes when the rough, firm voice of Yvonne confirmed his hopes and fears.

"So do you have anything to drink around here?"

He heard the sound of the refrigerator opening. "I have mineral water, cranberry juice, orange juice," Angelique replied.

"Orange juice? Really?" Yvonne asked. There was the sound of something thudding against flesh. "Where'd you get this?"

"Part of the perks of being an ambassador," Angelique replied. The refrigerator shut again. There was a silence. "So what do you want, Yvonne?"

"Damn, this is good!" Another pause. "I want to ask you if you enjoy your foreign work?" Yvonne finally said.

There was a creak and squeak as the chair behind the desk was moved and occupied. "Very much. Why; you want to make sure you take away the things I enjoy most when you become queen?" Angelique's voice was flat and direct.

"Quite the contrary, little sister. I would like you to become the minister of foreign affairs." Yvonne's voice had that drip of sweetness she'd used on rare occasions, and it made Jake twist a bit in his captor's grip.

"What's that?" Yvonne immediately asked. "Who's upstairs?"

"Shawn! Would you come down here, darling?" Angelique's voice was calm.

The man looked at Jake, then backed away. Jake just watched silently as the blond head disappeared below the floor. For a few seconds his mind flirted with the idea of crying out or crawling to the stairs, but he just stayed still, listening for the perfect time.

"What's this?" Yvonne asked. The sound of her boots meant that she must have been circling the man with her predatory glance.

"Who's this?" Angelique corrected. "This is Shawn, the companion I picked up in the California Republic."

"Companion? You mean slave," Yvonne stated. "Where's the collar, or don't they do that in California?"

"I did not misspeak," Angelique said. A silence followed.

"He can't be from a ruling family," Yvonne said.

"There are no ruling families with us," the man said.

Jake tensed as he heard the low growl in Yvonne's throat, a sign that she was displeased but controlling it. "Then you'd best remember that here we do have ruling families, and while here you will treat us with respect," she threatened.

"I meant no offense, your majesty," the man replied.

"Are you jealous, sister?" Angelique asked with a tinkle of laughter in her voice. "I take it from Father's comments that you have not found your slave?"

"Not yet, but it will be soon," Yvonne snapped.

"I'm surprised that it has taken so long. Over a week, isn't it?" Angelique added. "I am so disappointed in you, big sister."

"I need not impress you. It is you who must impress me," Yvonne replied. There was some silence and then the sound of glass clicking on wood. "Father is impressed with your diplomatic skills. I'm satisfied."

"What more do you want?" Angelique asked.

"Everything," Yvonne said with a chuckle. "Goodnight, little sister."

Jake sat up on the bed as the door closed below. He shook his head, sending the beads of sweat which had formed there flying. He looked up just as the man rose into the room via the staircase. After the gag was removed, he swallowed the spit that had built up in his mouth.

"Thank you for not making a scene," Angelique said as she passed the bed.

Jake turned his head to watch her disappear behind the hallway into the bathroom. His head swung back as he felt his hands untied. "Who are you?"

"I'm Shawn," the man said. He stood up straight and raised his hands in front of him. "Rub them like this; it will help the circulation," he instructed as he rubbed one wrist with the opposite palm, then switched. "Hope I didn't hurt you so much."

"He's had much worse, I'm sure," Angelique replied as she returned. Now dressed in green pajamas, she embraced the blond man. Her green eyes remained focused on Jake as she allowed her companion to hug and caress her for several minutes. "So what was he doing when you found him?" she asked as she very gently pushed the blond back.

"Going through the desk, like you knew he would," Shawn said as he rubbed the back of his neck. Against his groin the fabric of his simple pants

JUSTICE AND OTHER SHORT EROTIC TALES

had grown taut; the look in his eyes darkened as the princess approached Jake.

Jake moved back so that he was sitting on the edge of the bed as the princess joined him. She crossed her legs at the knees and placed one hand on his knee. "My desk, huh? Find anything of interest there?"

"Yeah, the refrigerator, the books," Jake began. He glanced up as the blond stepped behind the princess.

"I can tie him up for the night to make sure he doesn't run out and get your sister," Shawn suggested, his hands in fists as her hand slipped farther up Jake's leg.

Jake looked into her green eyes, which were dark and narrowed. His body tingled as her hand caressed his thigh. He screamed as she spun, and a line of red blocked his vision for a second. "What?" he cried out as he stepped back. His leg ached, and he saw a thin line of blood seeping through his pants.

"I, uh," the blond gargled as he dropped to his knees. Jake stepped back, clenching at his stomach as the man toppled over and a stream of blood flowed from his head.

Angelique turned to the slave and showed him the knife she had had hidden in her hand, under the pajama top. "I really hate jealousy," she said. "Folks who are jealous are rarely loyal. Disloyalty cannot be allowed; too dangerous."

Jake just stood there breathing heavily. He turned as she propelled him to the bed. He crawled underneath as directed and watched as she rang the servants' bell and spoke into the intercom. Soon several pairs of bare feet and one shod pair appeared from the direction of the slaves' entrance. The slaves pulled the body out then cleaned the floor quickly and silently.

Angelique's green eyes looked under the bed, her hair slapping down on the floor. "You may come out now. They're gone."

Jake raised himself from the floor after crawling out. The floor was perfectly clean; there was no sign of the murder that was just committed. "They'll tell my mistress," he whispered, then tensed for a slap which never came. When he glanced up the green eyes were twinkling back at him over a grin.

"That would be a choice – the incorrect choice," Angelique said. Her eyes slid down to his leg, causing her to frown. "You'd best take care of the leg," she instructed with a nod toward the bathroom. As he went in the direction indicated she called after him, "Keep your word, slave. I'm your owner now."

Jake paused, then bowed his body slowly, then rose again. "Yes, My Lady." After a few silent seconds he continued to the bathroom.

The cut wasn't deep, and the bleeding had already stopped. The material of the pants would need to be soaked, he realized, so he took them off. The antiseptic stung as he applied it and a bandage to the wound. No, the cut wasn't what hurt, really; it was the surprise that made him shake even now.

He jumped, knocking his knee into the sink, when Angelique's face appeared in the mirror.

"I thought you could use these," she simply stated, that smile on her face indicating that she was amused, as she tossed the brown pajamas to him.

She was gone before he could speak. Jake looked into the mirror at his emaciated frame after removing his shirt. *I look worse than when I first got here*, he thought as he recalled the month-plus of starvation in Yvonne's hyper-guarded suite.

The strong image of the heir to the throne came to his mind: always ready for combat, a weapon within easy reach, her hands quick to administer punishment. Her voice was firm, the statements plain and simple, the joy evident when she humiliated him, the tremble of flames underneath her words as she angered. Her body was firm and lean – barely anything extra on her – displayed to make a man or woman weak from desire and fear. She was every dark damned fantasy he'd ever had; she was a slow, passionate death.

A giggle broke the image and replaced it with the full-figured little sister, her hair tumbling around her shoulders, her eyes lighted by the hidden thoughts behind the laughter. Nothing like he'd dreamed of, except when he'd been talking with his gang back in the city, an image of femininity none of them could see in mothers or girlfriends. Her words were puzzles and questions mixed with statements that made his body tremble with fear and hope. A calmness echoing from each word, each step, each movement, shone from her. Around her there was a shadow he couldn't see past.

Jake splashed his face with cold water to clear his head. He checked out his section of the storage cabinet, noting that everything he expected was there. So far she hadn't touched him, and her earlier words returned to his mind. He took out the razor and touched up his face, then splashed a bit of cologne on before dressing.

She was in bed reading when he entered the bedroom. The covers were tossed back so she could lean over a large book laid out before her. As he approached he could see it was one of the picture books he'd found below the desk. "Is this what you were looking at when Shawn found you?"

"Yes, My Lady. You said I could look around. I didn't pick any locks," Jake added.

Angelique's head turned up. "I didn't read about any thieving skills in your record," she simply stated before turning the page. Her gaze returned to the book. "You recognize him," she said, tapping the page with one manicured fingernail.

Jake went to the side of the bed nearest her and bent over to see. "Shawn?" he asked, a bit surprised.

She nodded and turned the page several times, each page had the blond's picture on it. She stopped at the first blank page. "My collection," she sighed as she sat back and looked at the slave. She sniffed. "Cologne. Very nice."

Jake felt his body heat up at the compliment, his heartbeat thumping a bit louder in his ears. "You said I would get what I asked for, My Lady," he reminded her.

"Yes," Angelique agreed. She reached out and stroked his nearest hand. A chuckle rose in her throat as his cock poked up, expanding the pajamas. "Didn't my sister utilize her property?"

"Of course," Jake heard himself say, then cursed himself as he continued, "I miss that so much."

"You sound like you might be in love with her," Angelique sniffed.

Jake's body shook as the suggestion sent a wave of chill through him. "No, of course not," he answered. "She trained me very well," he added in a whisper.

There was silence for a few moments, then she paged back the picture book to a particularly enticing image. "Did you ever do this with her?"

"No, My Lady," he said. Instead of a teasing reply or a sharp order to go fetch materials, she simply closed the book. He looked up as the covers were moved and she slid between them.

"That's too bad," Angelique told him. She pointed to the end of the bed. "There's a bedroll for you. Time to go to sleep, Jake."

"Yes, My Lady," he said as he moved away. At the end of the bed was a thin mattress rolled up around a pillow and a blanket. It was soft even on the hard wooden floors. From there he could see the edge of the canopy in the starlight filtering through the windows.

No chains, no guards, no bars on the windows, her just a few feet away. Jake remembered the tiny slave cells he'd been shoved into and the room he'd shared with three half-siblings in a tenement house in the city. The feeling of shackles on him as he hung over the red and black silk covers made tears come to his eyes. *This is too much freedom.* His thoughts surprised him enough to make him sit up straight.

The promises the Butcher made and his days in the dungeon flooded his mind. Suddenly everywhere he looked he saw nothing but bars and traps. Beneath was the pulse his blood vibrated with as he remembered each torture, each touch, each orgasm he'd felt, really truly felt, for the first time with her. He sobbed as he lay back down.

It wasn't that there was a plot to take over the kingdom, Jake discovered, so much as a plan that could be put into action if need be. Each day there was a meeting between Angelique, Corriger, and several household servants and staff. Among these he was surprised to see the woman doctor, the girl Betty from the kitchen, and even the chief stablehand. He learned from the doctor that Yvonne had gone back on several promises made to each of them.

Phone calls came in as well which made Angelique nod and take down notes that only Corriger was allowed to see. Jake stood in the office off to one side during all of this, his presence ignored most of the time. Every now and then Angelique would direct a question toward him. Usually these were about Yvonne's daily habits, the number of weapons that might be hidden out of sight in her room, things which they thought someone who had been so close to her might know that General Corriger apparently did not.

Jake would answer as completely as he could, though he felt he was the biggest Judas in the world while he did so. The words of a man who'd claimed to be his father would ring in his ears: "If you're going to hell already, what does one more sin matter?" Other words Yvonne herself drilled into him made each piece of information he gave feel like a knife: "You don't exist except for me, slave."

With each day that passed his image in the bathroom mirror grew firmer and healthier, making the Butcher's words less real. Then he'd remember the number of troops and loyal guards Yvonne controlled. According to the staff and slaves that number seemed to be lessening but was still huge. On one such day, as he stood in the bathroom after a particularly tiring meeting, he sighed and stepped back from the mirror and into the shower to clean up.

About an hour later he presented himself nude to Angelique, a coil of rope he'd found in her clothes closet in his hands. "My Lady," he began, he still could not say the words he sensed she truly wanted. The old brand with Yvonne's particular twist on the royal crest had been removed a few days after he was introduced to the younger princess, but Yvonne's implanted status still burned in every cell of his body.

Angelique looked up from the statue she was holding. She smiled, then held it toward him. "There are many paths for each of us," she said as she touched the hands of the figure. "Each one based on our desires, on our means, on our ability. But they should also be based on knowledge, because, once chosen, the path determines which choices are available next."

She set the statue down, then crossed to sit on the end of her bed. "Why did you become a drug dealer, Jake?"

The slave blinked and stepped back. Here he was, offering himself to her in a way he had thought would please her, and she asked him such a non-erotic question. It didn't take more than a minute for him to come up with an answer. "I've always desired to be a slave. That was a way to get my desires."

Angelique tilted her head, then shook it. "Really? Are you sure you're not just repeating what my dear sister wished to hear?"

"The law is the law," he began, sudden doubts rising in his mind. "I knew the law; I knew the consequences. I made a choice, My Lady, and I got what I deserved."

"True," Angelique agreed with the last statement. "That doesn't answer my question, however." Instead of pressing for further conversation she stood up and took the rope from him. "Now you will get some knowledge."

Jake looked down at the web of white rope that bound him between the two rings hanging from the ceiling. He could barely feel it touching him, and none of it was tight, yet he couldn't move a muscle beyond his head, fingers, and toes.

Angelique had shed her clothing and was standing looking at him. Her skin glistened with perspiration from her hours of work. She lifted her braids and fastened them on top of her head with two large pins.

Jake's cock grew as much as it could, wrapped as it was in the coil of rope and pulled back toward his own ass. He watched her breasts lift as she worked with her hair, then bounce slightly, the pectoral muscles giving them a firm shape as she lowered her arms. Swallowing, he allowed himself to speak his thoughts. "You are so beautiful, My Lady."

Her lips smiled and parted as her tongue darted out to lick them. This seduction was completely unlike anything he had experienced. She need not have played to his visual senses, for her word and the fear that he could be killed at any moment would have been enough to have him between her legs. As her tongue made a round circuit of her full lips her eyes swept over his body. "Very nice work," she told herself as she moved closer.

Jake sighed as he felt the heat from her body rush around him. Her hands sent jolts through his flesh even when they touched merely the rope. At some point he had become the rope, the rope being his only means of standing on his feet as his body went limp with desire, the rope, and therefore himself, her instrument, subtle and strong like herself. He gasped as she jerked his head back with his hair. The expected blade never met his throat, but her wet, coarse tongue traveled over the skin of one ear and then of the other. His gasps grew as her teeth pulled at one lobe.

"I think you like that," she whispered as she withdrew. She chuckled as Jake jerked his body in an attempt to regain contact with her. "Ah, but you offered yourself. Now you must accept the consequences," she reminded him. "Or must you?" she teased as she pinched a free inch of flesh on his buttocks.

"Yes," Jake gasped. He moaned as his cheeks, already parted by the rope, were shoved further apart by a wet digit. Weeks of disuse after months of constant torment made his body ache at the thought of what might happen next.

"Do you give yourself to me, Jake, or do I take it from you?" she whispered, adding a second finger inside of him.

In Jake's mind his body seemed to shrink down to the area around his asshole. The ropes seemed non-existent, her fingers his only support. He heard the question repeated, so he replied in words mixed with gasps as the feelings pulled him within himself. "Take it, Jake is yours, My Lady," he cried out.

A sigh was his only reply as the fingers were pulled out and the ropes once more formed his world. Jake turned his head and saw Angelique wipe her hands before pulling on a robe. He watched, his mouth opened, the words to plead for anything on his lips, as she moved to stand in front of him.

The words he said made little difference as she untied and expertly recoiled the ropes. While the setup had taken a few hours, the removal was far quicker, and soon Jake was swaying a bit at the pressure his body placed on his legs. Angelique's eyes were pale as she shook her head at him, tossed the rope onto her bed, and walked away.

"My Lady. What did your slave do?" he began as he took two steps forward, then started to fall. He balanced himself on one knee and his hands, watching her retreat down the hallway. "Mistress," he whispered; the word still caught in his chest. He shook his head as he lowered himself to the ground.

Jake rubbed his body, which was covered with gooseflesh from the lack of blood to all his body but his cock and balls. Turning toward the window he blinked and held his breath. The air was chilly because the glass was thrown back, the curtains billowing in the night breeze.

He stood up and went to the balcony and out into the darkness. The moon above was a crescent of faded yellow against the points of white twinkling around it. Never had he been allowed out on the Butcher's balcony, not even after he had been certain he had proved his loyalty. His cock, which should have been withering in the cool breeze, brushed against his thigh as it grew.

He could leave, take that rope lying on the bed and climb down, run out into the night and away from the insanity that would break out as soon as the king died. The world was so much larger than he had realized. Then a figure on a horse below caught his eye, and he backed against the wall. The Butcher dismounted, slapped the stable boy twice, then stormed into the palace and out of sight. His cock should have been bursting now, but instead it had retreated in fear.

"I wonder if you can understand?" Angelique's voice behind him made Jake turn. She was dressed in her pajamas, her hair loose around her shoulders.

Jake looked down at his bare feet, then back up at the princess. "I don't think I do," he said, pleading silently for the answers that would take him from hiding and bind him to her.

"I won't tell you what to think. I'm not her," Angelique said.

Corriger, however, was neither as kind nor as concerned with Jake's humanity. She was having enormous fun dictating how and when Jake and Ann would amuse themselves and the free women. On any of the previous nights Jake would have begged for any type of sexual contact, but Angelique hadn't responded to his offers. Now in the middle of the fourth forced fuck with Ann he was wishing it would end, as was the slave girl.

Corriger and her slave had come to Angelique's office late with several sealed envelopes. The contents had greatly upset the princess, and she gone on a rampage for almost an hour. The documents were copies of drafts for new laws Yvonne would issue after the king's death, a loss that seemed certain to occur before the week ended. Each law, in the youngest princess' words, "immorally infringed on the rights of citizens." The proposed changes included expanding the enslavement penalty to the offspring of those convicted if born after sentence was passed, confiscation of property as a penalty for discussion and trade with enemies of the state, which meant any nation not having a treaty with the United Lands, and state control over all video media.

After literally breaking the window in her office with her fist, Angelique had been forced to retire to her bedroom by Corriger. To calm the princess, Corriger directed the two slaves to put on a good show, primarily consisting of Jake's performing various sexual acts on Ann. The slave girl seemed to enjoy the attention at first, but as he offered his cock to her mouth for the third time Jake could see tears forming in her eyes.

"I can't do this," Jake announced as he pulled away and stood up.

"You will until I decide otherwise!" Corriger ordered in a yell that made Ann cringe in terror.

"It's hurting her!" Jake replied as he picked his clothes up from the floor. "If you want to hurt her, you do it; I won't."

Corriger rose to her feet, swaying a bit from the alcohol she'd been consuming during the show. "You're forcing me to hurt her, slave! Do you enjoy seeing her beaten in front of you?"

"Jake, please," Ann whispered as she was pulled up by her hair.

His heart pounding, Jake knelt before the princess. "My Lady, please," he begged.

Angelique's faded eyes looked at him from under the hand she'd had over her eyes for the last several minutes. "General, take your girl and leave. I have a headache," the princess added before Corriger could object.

"As you wish, Your Majesty," Corriger replied as she released her slave by shoving her toward her own pile of clothing on the floor. "I'm sorry you were not calmed by these two."

Angelique just nodded and stood up with a wave toward the door.

Jake watched as the general steered Ann out the door, the slave girl clenching her clothing to her body. Once the door was closed behind them he looked up at the princess. "Thank you, My Lady."

"I do have a headache," Angelique said.

"Is there anything your slave can do to ease it?" Jake asked as he sat up on his knees.

The princess merely sighed, shaking her head, then walked toward the bathroom. Jake stayed on his knees for a few moments, trying to figure everything out. He gave up when he caught the multi-armed goddess regarding him with what now seemed like a sad smile. Some days he would have sworn that statue was alive since the little face seemed to hold every imaginable expression.

Jake's cock ached as he pulled his pants off, not from arousal but from over-use. *That's something I never thought could happen,* he thought as he put his pajamas on. He considered the canopied bed after donning the pajama top. The sound of the shower ended as he made a decision. The bed sheets were soft, but not satin as Yvonne's had been. He folded down a corner on the side she'd been sleeping on and stacked the quilt at the foot of the bed. He'd just finished laying out his own bedding when Angelique tapped him on the shoulder.

"Thank you," she simply said with a tired smile.

The slave nodded. After the princess was in bed, the covers tucked around her so that one arm rested outside and the other cradled her head, Jake knelt at the edge. "Is there nothing your slave can do for you, My Lady?"

"You could call me Mistress," Angelique said. She waved him away when he could only open and close his mouth a few times without success. "She still owns you. How very sad."

Jake blinked. He waited a few moments as he gazed upon her face, her closed eyes and tiny sleepy expression making her seem far more fragile that he knew she was. He crawled to the end of the bed and lay down himself. As his hand brushed his cock when he scratched his thigh, he noted with amazement that it was hard again. Odd, because he didn't really feel aroused in any usual way. He decided it was just his body betraying him, something he should have been used to after months with the Butcher. That thought, however, made him limp and eager for sleep.

The next three days were devoted to more meetings, with Jake's role further reduced to fetching drinks for people and answering the slaves' entrance when food was brought. At first, he'd flattered himself into thinking that the atrocities that Yvonne was accused of were a result of losing him. But the list reached back farther, to before he had even been enslaved. Her pleasure in torturing him was not unique. Her excursions into the cities had been for pleasure, and the reported drafts of her new laws proved that she intended to continue to rule with an iron fist.

Nothing was ever said about what the Butcher had done to her sister to earn the dangerous hatred that blazed behind those green eyes whenever Jake found Angelique looking at pictures of the royal family. It was true that Jake himself had been the final cause of Corriger's dismissal, but the general had complaints galore and very few compliments. Betty and the chief stablehand had come into the conspiracy last, after Yvonne had sent away Mike, the promised husband for the kitchen maid, for no reason, it was reported.

Jake was standing off in one corner just listening when a call came. Angelique told everyone to stay where they were, and soon they were joined by the chief steward. The man barely gave Jake a second glance, nor did he seem surprised to find Corriger standing next to the princess. Jake couldn't believe the words coming from the steward's mouth.

"The Queen Mother has sent me to you, Princess Angelique, to inform you of His Majesty the King's death." The entire room was quiet as Angelique moved around her desk, motioning for the steward to continue. "The Queen Mother wishes to know when you will be moving against your sister."

"What are you talking about, old man?" Corriger began until Angelique held up her hand.

"Is there proof?" the princess simply asked.

The chief steward nodded and returned to the door. The doctor who had primarily cared for Jake entered now, carrying a folder in her hand. "I have the test results," the doctor said.

Angelique took the offered documents and read them, then handed them to Corriger. "How do you know she arranged this?"

The doctor grew very pale, but she spoke with only a slight quiver in her voice. "I gave her the poison myself. I told her how to administer it. Just as you instructed."

Jake took the folder from the chief stablehand and looked at the enclosed blood tests. The king had died of hemorrhaging. There were medical terms he couldn't understand, but the conversation indicated that Yvonne was to blame.

Angelique put her arm around the doctor's shoulder. "You'll be taken care of, my dear doctor. Don't worry. Just be patient."

"She must know," the doctor responded. "She knows everything that goes on around here. She'll kill us all."

"So she'll kill us a little sooner than she would have anyway," Corriger stated. She turned to Jake with narrowed eyes and a cocked grin. "Or a little later for others."

No one said anything as Jake bolted up the staircase. The balcony doors were open, and he sought refuge there. The dark night was pierced over and over by crying and screaming, and by bells tolling the death of the king. On every television set the announcement would be made. At first there would be riots and parties in the street, the poor people celebrating a slight victory by simply surviving their oppressors. The announcements of Yvonne's succession would end all such celebrations very soon.

Jake ignored the chilly breeze as he leaned over the rail. Corriger had, of course, been correct. He would die soon. The collar felt as though it was choking him, so he pushed one finger between it and his throat. He had begged her for death once, he had accepted it hanging in the dungeon, and now he looked down from the fourth floor, wondering if the fall would be a quick ending. His fingers pulled on his collar and he swore into the darkness. He couldn't even jump, because his body belonged to someone else. Instead he cursed himself and went to the bathroom.

Angelique had given him permission to use the bathroom whenever he wished, so he used that privilege now in an attempt to wash away the fear. Each time he closed his eyes, the image of cruel eyes and shoulder-length scarlet hair filled his mind, and behind them the words he'd burned into his mind. *Jake doesn't exist except for you*. Jake washed himself slowly, no longer trying to block the memories he had been blocking ever since his failed attempt to seduce the younger princess.

The water fell over his body; the soap slipped upon his flesh. The razor tingled his skin as he carefully shaved each spot he could reach. Each day without fail he had used everything in the personal hygiene bag, and tonight he used them again. The enema reminded him of the thrill he had felt as Yvonne had watched him from her tub. He could almost picture her through the curtains, except these were not clear but mint green, and the bathtub was behind a screen.

His wrists ached as he reached up and placed his hands around the spout where they had been chained on many occasions. Holding himself in place, he could imagine how trapped he had felt, how aroused and how alive the vibrating dildo in his ass had made him feel on such occasions. Jake thrust forward and felt the heavy bounce of his cock. He sighed and rolled his head against one arm.

A chill swept over him, and his mind was dark. His hands were no longer holding the shower spout but were chained; the water was no longer hitting him, just drops that sounded in the darkness, Yvonne's voice in his head repeated a different sentence: *I'll just kill you when I tire of you*. He jumped back and found his hands at his sides, the tiles of the bathtub still around him, and the mint green curtain to one side. His cock hung firm and heavy until he pounded his head against the tiles.

"I hope you haven't broken anything." Angelique's voice made Jake turn around. Her head was poking through the far end of the curtain, looking at him with a sad frown. "Remembering good times or bad?" she asked.

"Both," Jake replied. He lowered his eyes, then raised them again. "Do you wish anything, My Lady?" he asked.

Angelique tilted her head before replying. "You wish to go back to her, don't you?"

Jake closed his eyes. *I'm a fool, a complete fool*, he told himself as he remained silent. He opened his eyes as the shower floor moved a bit to find her climbing naked into the shower. The tiles felt cool as he backed up as far as he could.

"You were fantasizing about her taking you back, correct?" Angelique asked as she stepped onto the tiny mint green fish that were pressed into the bottom of the shower to stop slips. "What were you thinking? What was she doing to you?"

"It was, kind of, a memory," Jake said slowly.

"I want to know," Angelique said as she moved under the stream of water, so close to him that he could smell the perfume she wore being washed away. Her hand grabbed his wrist and held it fast. "It had something to do with your wrists."

"Yes, My Lady. She handcuffed me to the showerhead and did whatever she wished to this body," he said as he looked at her fingernails. Her grip was firm but relaxed, her presence was calm and sure, and his breathing increased rapidly.

"And in your fantasy just now she did the same thing because she was so happy to have you back?"

"Yes, but . . ." Jake tried to pull his hand free, but found her grasp to be as strong as always. "I'd end up back in the dungeon on my way to death again."

"You still want to go back to her?" Angelique asked as she released his hand.

"She is my mistress still," he said, then jerked back as though she would strike him. The green eyes just regarded him seriously and quietly. "I wish it wasn't so," Jake added as he bowed his head. He sighed as fingers crept through his wet hair, combing it out and patting his head.

"What do you wish was so?" Angelique whispered into the ear her caressing had uncovered.

Images ran through Jake's mind. A bigger apartment than the tenement he had been raised in was something he had had for a while. Rolls of hundreds in his pocket had become a reality. The look of fear in people's eyes when he told them the price had just increased. The desperate moaning of a woman screwing for a gram or two of whatever he was dealing at the moment. The feeling of the whip as it caught him on his ribs and the pressure as his ass was fucked. Each one of these had something he wanted or thought he wanted or had been told he wanted.

He raised his eyes and looked into hers. *Everyone has choices. I won't tell you what to think.* His knees felt weak; his body was both icy and burning at the same time. "May I please be excused, My Lady?" he begged with a whimper in his voice.

Angelique stepped back and pointed to the curtain. "You're not worth it," she said softly.

Jake blinked, then hurried from the shower and bathroom. Out on the balcony he cursed himself once more. He looked at the statue underneath the staffs near the balcony where Angelique prayed each morning. Each hand represented a choice and a path, each path branching off into other choices, both our own and others she had explained to him when he had asked.

After a few minutes he went to the door and tried the knob. It turned in his hands, and the door opened back into the bedroom suite. He was completely nude; the water had dried on his body, but his hair was still damp. Angelique didn't appear to tell him to stop or to tackle him, Corriger wasn't waiting outside for him. Jake stepped out onto the hallway carpet and closed the door behind him. The lock clicked, and he realized there was only one place for him to go now.

Yvonne barely looked up when he walked into her office on the other side of the palace. She glanced at him once, then sat back in her chair and returned her attention to the document she'd signed only minutes before.

Jake swallowed, then lowered himself to the floor, his arms and legs flat. Her boots appeared in front of his face a few minutes later. At her order he raised himself enough to lick them thoroughly. The texture beneath his lips, the taste of leather and dust, made him hard as he put all his attentions into them. He yelped when she grasped his hair and lifted him up to his knees.

"So, did my little sister treat you all right, slave?" Yvonne asked. She smiled when his face clouded with fear and surprise. "Oh, yes, I've known where you've been this entire time. Haven't I, Ann?"

Jake's eyes narrowed as the slave girl walked down the spiral staircase from the bedroom above. She was naked, her body marked with red welts and scratches, and Jake felt his cock shrink as any pity he had felt was replaced by anger. Ann moved to Yvonne's side and laid her head on the new queen's arm. "Yes, Mistress. Your slave hopes you are happy."

"No!" Jake screamed as he tried to stand up. His efforts ended with his lip bleeding from the blow the Butcher's hand dealt him. The force had thrown him against a wall. "Your slave has returned to you, Mistress," he said as he rose to his knees.

"Yes, but you're not interesting any more," Yvonne said. She grabbed the slave girl by her smooth pubes, smiling as she cried out and opened her legs wider. "Now Ann, here, is much more interesting than you could ever be, drug dealer."

Jake fought the tears that were building up in his eyes, threatening to blind him. He reached for the doorknob and was forced back by the shock he received.

"It's too late, slave," Yvonne said. She slapped Ann's ass, and the slave girl ran up the staircase. "But don't worry. I'll give you my full attention right after I've taken care of a few last-minute things."

Jake sobbed as he rubbed his burned hands. He looked up as Yvonne stood over him. "Ah, did you think you'd be forgiven? Sorry, you committed the crime; I'm merely carrying out justice," she said with a chuckle. "Something so many of my people have forgotten about lately. But that will change very soon."

Yvonne smiled as she noted that his cock was hard and edging up his stomach at the mere sight of her and the sound of her voice. She stepped very close and placed one boot between his legs, lifting his balls up with the tip of her foot.

Jake's breath caught in his throat as the feeling of leather and the power radiating from her overcame him. He pressed his lips together firmly to keep from begging, but a moan was building as she teased him by lowering and raising her foot.

"You'd come right now if I ordered you," Yvonne declared. She pulled her foot back and chuckled. "But I'm not going to."

Jake looked up and watched as she went up the staircase. Wrapping his arms around his bent legs he cursed himself as he rocked back and forth. He'd only had a few hours of sleep when the Butcher kicked him awake in the morning.

Jake stood still as the executions continued. First there had been the slaves and staff that had taken part in the conspiracy. None of them had begged for their lives, and most had cursed the new queen as she motioned and each head was severed. The Queen Mother sat on her throne in chains, Yvonne announcing that her mother would be allowed to live out her life in her room under guard after she saw what her foolishness had wrought and the number of deaths it was causing.

Most of the aristocracy had not been caught yet, but Jake had been forced to watch as the television announcements of rewards for their capture went out over the airways. Corriger walked up to the bloody block and spat toward Ann. Jake swallowed as the ax descended. His own death wouldn't be so easy, he was sure.

"Now for the final one of the day," Yvonne announced as she stood up.

Jake put his hands on his stomach as the younger princess was led out in chains. Though dressed in pajamas and slippers, just as she would have been after her shower, Angelique looked calm and certain of herself. Her eyes gazed directly at him and winked, causing Jake to blink in confusion.

"Do you so fear me, Your Majesty, that you must entrust my death to your guards?" Angelique asked calmly.

Yvonne stepped down to the floor. "Fear you? You stupid little bitch. I've known what you've been doing for years. I allowed you to do it."

"Ah, I see," Angelique said with a sad grin. "Then I think it only right you control everything, don't you?"

"No, you cannot. She is your sister!" the Queen Mother shouted. Jake rushed to protect the older woman who had had a few kind words for him but was thrown back by the guard, who slapped her down.

Yvonne turned toward the throne with a glare. "No one touches him but me!" Her eyes widened as the chains that linked her sister's wrists together suddenly encircled her throat.

Jake grabbed the traitor slave girl Ann and held her as she tried to join in the fight. "You little bitch; you lied to everyone, didn't you?" he growled as he forced her hands behind her back.

Angelique was strong, and her attack was unexpected, but it took Yvonne only a minute to toss her over her shoulder to land with a crunch across the bottom step leading to the thrones. The three red braids splayed out around her head, but there was no sound or movement. "I'll take you out, then, if that is your wish, little sister," Yvonne said as she took the ax from the executioner.

Jake pushed the slave girl to the floor and jumped down two steps. "Mistress, please!" he yelled, not knowing what to offer or to say but only thinking to delay things.

Yvonne glared up from where she'd crouched beside her sister. "Shut up!" Yvonne's eyes widened suddenly as she jerked her head upward. From her throat a dagger was sprouting, the red blood gushing out onto the carpet. She opened her mouth, but nothing issued forth but more blood.

"Release me!" the Queen Mother ordered, and after a moment the guards obeyed with mumbled apologies.

Angelique sat up, one hand to her head, and considered the body of her sister lying beside her. "Keys?" she asked suddenly.

Jake took the keys from the chief guard and hurried down. As he unlocked the shackles he kept looking at the Butcher, lying as she had laid out so many people before.

"She's quite dead," Angelique assured him. "I don't miss my mark. Thank you for giving me the distraction, Jake."

The slave looked into the new Queen's green eyes, then lowered his own. "What will you do with your slave?" he asked.

The green eyes went very cold, and the words spoken were like spears through his soul. "I haven't decided if I want him." Then she smiled and used him as a brace to help her stand. "Right now, I just want something to drink."

As they passed the weeping slave girl the new Queen stopped and wrapped an arm around the slim shaking shoulders. With her other hand she caressed the long brown hair. "Oh, Ann, you've become a traitor. I, of course, understand that Corriger mistreated you, and like a fool you thought my sister would treat you better. But even a slave must be loyal. And you've proved yourself disloyal."

Jake swallowed as he watched Angelique take the slave girl's head firmly in her hands. With one twist the sounds of Ann's weeping were cut short, as was her life. The new Queen sighed as she released the body, a look of exhaustion on her face. Jake simply stepped over the dead body and followed her out of the throne room to check on the condition of the palace.

That night as they watched the remaining slaves and staff clean up the throne room, Jake sat at the Queen's feet. Angelique touched her sister's throne announcing it was to be burnt. He held her goblet for her without being ordered to, pouring her more when she returned it to him.

When she returned the goblet for a third time he set it aside and moved so he was kneeling with his head to her slipper-shod feet. "Your slave is sorry and begs your forgiveness," he stated.

"Who?" Angelique asked.

Jake frowned and lifted himself up onto his hands. "Your slave, Mistress," he said.

"That would be my choice," Angelique pointed out. "So who, really, is sorry, and what is he sorry for? I can't make a choice without information."

"You know everything about me," Jake began. "Where I grew up, the fact that I dealt drugs for years, that I've been a slave for over five, almost six years now. That's all there is to me, just a slave, after being the lowest of the low," he said.

She just looked at him. Jake groaned and stood up. "Damn! What do you want? Do you want to hear my life story in detail? Do you want me to say I'm sorry that I dealt drugs? Well, my life story is pretty much the same as any poor kid's. And as for dealing and selling, I never forced anyone to buy; they all came to me looking for an escape. I'm sorry that some of them got hurt more in the process, but I never really thought about them. Just about having a roof over my own head and food in my own mouth and a little power now and then."

Angelique stood up. "You're telling me that you didn't have very many choices?" Her voice had a hard edge to it as she spoke.

"They were all bad choices," Jake said. "I just chose the worst of the lot."

"So what are you sorry for?" Angelique demanded as she stepped down to stand toe-to-toe with him.

Jake swallowed. "I'm sorry that I couldn't live up to my promise to you."

The green eyes blinked. "But you did. You obeyed me well, as well as you could, I think."

"I returned to your sister," Jake pointed out.

"I never said you couldn't; I simply asked that you obey me as your owner," Angelique replied. She placed one finger against her lips and considered him silently for a moment. "You are a slave by conviction for your crimes. You have served this nation by helping us rid ourselves of a grave threat to all our freedoms and lives. Therefore, I offer you a choice."

The Queen clapped her hands, and soon the guards entered with a cleaned-up and cared-for Queen Mother and the aristocrats, who'd returned upon word of the Butcher's death. "Jake Monroe, you may go free and leave this country, or you may choose to serve out your life in servitude for your crimes. This will be your final sentence as witnessed by these good folk," she announced loudly.

Jake shifted his weight from one leg to another. "As your slave?" he whispered.

"Of course; you are part of the inheritance," Angelique simply said.

Jake looked around at the faces of the guards and still-frightened aristocracy until his eyes met the Queen Mother's. He turned back then knelt down and looked up at the young Queen. "I wish to remain a slave," he said clearly.

Angelique nodded and clapped her hands again. The blacksmith who'd collared him before entered. His golden collar was removed with metal cutters and then replaced with a thicker one of silver. Each swallow he took made the metal rise and fall. His cock swelled as his head was pushed down by her bedroom slipper. "This slave is mine. No one else may command him but me. Is that understood?"

The crowd murmured their agreement. "Stand up, slave," Angelique ordered when the crowd has dispersed.

Jake rose and focused his gaze over his owner's shoulder. He blinked as her arms moved around him.

"Slave, carry me upstairs now," Angelique said. She sighed as her slave lifted her up into his arms, her back resting against one arm and the other supporting her legs, while hers wrapped around his neck. She turned his head toward her before he stepped out of the throne room. "I'm not my sister," she repeated.

"Mistress?" Jake asked as he looked into her eyes. His entire body was on fire; his pants were ready to burst, and oddly the fear that usually edged everything he had ever done in his life was slipping away with each second their eyes locked onto each other.

"I hope I don't have to tell you what to do once we're upstairs," Angelique said. "If I have to detail every little thing, I'll get bored," she further explained.

The threat was there simply because of her status and his. Underneath it all, she might not be all that different from Yvonne, but only time would tell that. Jake licked his lips. "Would I be allowed to ask questions?" he ventured.

Angelique giggled and tossed her head back so that the bandage on her forehead was visible for just a moment. "Of course," she replied. "You can't make good choices without good information. And there will be choices you'll have to make. Those will determine how you are treated."

"Then I hope I choose well, Mistress," Jake replied with a smile and a twinkle in his eyes.

They were up in her suite in a few minutes. Jake laid her on the bed, then stepped back. He slowly removed his clothing, turning his body so she could see everything she now owned. He removed her slippers first so he could lavish his attentions there. He sucked and licked each of her toes until she giggled and pulled back.

Her breasts were as full and soft as he'd imagined them to be. He eagerly put his lips to each nipple and sucked it to a hard little point. Then he turned to her neck as she lifted it up and back. Her gasps seemed far more real than any he had heard before, and their sound made him harder than he had ever been. Free to do what he wanted to please her, he traveled down her stomach, taut with muscle, and lowered her pants with her assistance.

One glance up into her wide eyes made the permission he was about to ask for irrelevant. He drove between her thighs and worked at the slits and crevasses there. When her thighs grasped his head he took her offered hands and held them as she rolled from one orgasm into another for minutes. He wiped his wet face on the bedding as she settled back down into a relaxed state.

When Angelique touched his head he looked up, expecting a slap or a harsh word. "That was very good, slave," she said.

"Thank you, Mistress," Jake replied. He helped her crawl under the bedcovers, got her a half glass of water, and then went to lay out his mattress at the end of the bed.

Jake never thought to beg for an orgasm himself, and Angelique never offered or teased him. By choice he was her slave, and by choice she had accepted him. That path meant that other choices were no longer options for either one of them. In the moonlight, the statue of the many-armed goddess on the altar seemed to smile.

The Flesh Is Weak

I SET MY COFFEE DOWN AND LOOK AT THE wisps of steam drifting up from it. My agent, Susan, is still talking about the report on sales of my latest book, but my mind isn't focusing on her words. My mind isn't focusing on the cafe, my mind isn't even focusing on my fingernails as I try very hard to see every line in them.

I can still hear his voice, his pleading and then the threats, and then the crying and more threats. The call from the hospital surfaces in my mind next. "I'm not his girlfriend or his wife," I recall saying. After the nurse insisted for a few minutes, I was headed toward the emergency ward. He was lying there in bed with straps holding him down on the bed and tiny lines delivering medicine, nutrients, and pain killers to him. I could have told them that the last he didn't require. He smiled in that sad manipulative way and spoke to me. "See, I can't live without you, Mistress. You are my life."

Yeah right. That's why I had ended up in the hospital with broken ribs a month before. The latest stunt was his undoing, because the courts now tagged him and forbade him from being within a half-kilometer of me. Of course, I have to carry a tag as well and have a monitor installed in my home, but at least he is gone from my life.

"That sounds great," I mumble as I try to join the conversation in progress.

Susan tilts her head to one side and shakes it. "You haven't a clue what I said, do you?"

"Sure, my next project, something for television," I reply, the words she spoke vaguely forming images in my mind.

"So you wouldn't mind being head writer for a show about a sexually-frustrated bowl of oatmeal?" she says.

"What?" I ask as I sit up and frown at her.

"See, you weren't listening," Susan replies. "I could tell you were gone." She leans forward and places her well-manicured hand over one of mine. "So, you were back at the hospital again?"

Sometimes I wish she were just my agent and not my best friend. This is one of those times.

"It's been three years, Leslie. You must move on," Susan tells me, echoing my therapist, my mother, and my own common sense.

I nod and hear myself explain. "It isn't easy. I'm not as easily pleased as you. I'm more complicated, you know." This is our public way of saying we both know I'm kinky to the core and could never have that little house with the white picket fence, the cats and the kids. At least, not unless the father was also my property.

By now it's supposed to be easier. With the death of the religious conservative movement, after the environmental and political crises of the early twenty-first century, a new world of opportunities and rights began. One of these was the birth of dozens if not hundreds of types of legally-recognized unions between human beings. All it takes is two consenting adults, a contract, and a judge. But there are no classes to teach people what each type of common union entails, and so folks still lie in order to get what they really want. I vaguely remember someone predicting this from a history class I took in college. I'm living proof that they were correct.

"I've tried," I begin. "I've rejoined all the organizations; I've even gone to a few parties. There is nothing there for me. All this freedom has just increased the fakiness. I want reality."

Susan is wonderful; she doesn't understand my own interests firsthand, but she knows what has made me happy and what has created the best work from me. She clicks on her computer for a few moments, then smiles at me. "You want your fantasies to become reality. But that's not reality. The fact that you have to publish or perish, that you have to pay taxes, that we all have to be born and die. That's reality. You don't need to go to a club for that."

I roll my eyes as Susan continues. Somewhere I'm vaguely aware that she disapproves of my interests but is far too wise to say it. I am her biggest client after all, aside from the friendship that is.

"And in order to live, you have to work, which is where I am of assistance," Susan states. She learns forward now, all business in her demeanor. "Take the proposal I have from Moonlight. They want to do an erotic series with aliens, androids, cyborgs, even ghosts and all sorts of paranormal stuff."

"And that's what you want me to write?" I ask as I wrinkle up my nose. Personally, my erotica has always followed my more mainstream fiction, historicalnovels based on research and my useless college degrees. "I don't do science fiction," I began to say.

"Actually, they don't want you to write. You'll be the senior consultant on relationships, historical facts, kinky stuff." Susan takes some paper from her briefcase and hands it to me. "Here is what they are offering and all the details. If you want to write a episode, they want it, but no pressure."

"But I don't do science fiction; I don't do horror," I repeat.

"Look, you've made over three million with your books, and that's just the erotica; if you add the historical fiction that figure triples. You write what you know, people, and then you just fit them into a stable place and a situation." Susan shuts down her computer and returns it to her briefcase. "Audiences are tired of the mindless special effects and the lame one-dimensional characters. Your sales are proof of that, Leslie. Moonlight is willing to pay well."

"I'll think it over, then, but no guarantees," I finally say. The rest of our meal is spent on her trying to convince me to come with her and her spouse to the mountains this weekend. I decline and mumble that my next book is waiting for me back at my place.

My place is an estate out in the country. A large, two story earth home on twenty acres of land with an artificial pond and passive solar power. The perfect house only because I bought it after the nightmare, imperfect because the remnants are still terrorizing my mind.

Another message from my last ex is on my answering machine. Is it any wonder that everything I write nowadays is about war-torn romance, the sadistic dictator and the manipulated heroine who manages to save herself and those around her? I'm trying to recreate my own life in the words on my screen, trying to make life out of the ashes left behind.

Once I told myself that I could live without the fakiness; I could survive on my books, on my fantasies. I swore off the clubs and the chat rooms, the mailing lists and the organizations. Until I met Frank. He seemed perfect, especially when I ignored the fact that he needed to constantly be within my line of sight, which of course meant that I always had to be within his. It was just devotion, I told myself, and isn't that what everyone wants from a slave? He signed everything over to me and moved in. He was there with my favorite meals and took care of me when I was sick. He made sure the creeps stayed away from me when we were at parties and clubs. I was making the scene again, and folks seemed so happy to see me.

Until Frank broke a guy's nose. That was the first time I'd seen him hurt someone, and at the time I felt wonderful. He was my knight in shining armor, jumping up from his knees to defend me. I didn't even notice that I was getting sick more often until Susan asked me why the book was taking so long. Frank loved to take care of me when I was sick. He'd bring me in the best food, and entertain me with books or movies. He never left my side.

He was very angry when I went on a trip alone with Susan to a writer's retreat. That was the first time he raised his voice to me. He said, "Who will take care of you? Why do you deny me my job, my life?" He called me every day while I was gone.

After a week at the retreat I felt completely well. In the back of my mind I now realized that I knew something wasn't right. The fact that I felt better and that Susan had arranged for me to see a doctor at the retreat only brought my subconscious fears to the surface. The blood tests at the beginning of the retreat and the day before I left proved that I was being poisoned. I wanted to go back to my apartment where Frank was waiting for me, but Susan wouldn't let me.

It is commonly preached that tops have all the power because they wield the whip. But obsession has no scene role. And devotion can be just a cover for domination. The realization made me ill in more ways than one, and I contacted my lawyer and ended the contract immediately. I thought that after I returned all of his former possessions and his name to him that it would be over. Real life isn't that easy.

So now I'm sitting here reading over the contract from Moonlight. Perhaps it was time to give up on reality or at least open myself up to other options. Just buying a new house hasn't helped, and changing my phone number isn't the safety I was hoping for. I call Susan, and she is thrilled by my decision. Then I call the police and report Frank. When they call back in an hour, he's in custody again. I throw out all my whips, my canes, and the kinky books; my own I box up and take to the storage room. I'll make a new life for myself, "free and clear" as they say.

Three years later the series is a big success; in fact, I'm at a party celebrating our third Emmy award when Susan approaches me. I smile back weakly as she hugs and releases me then turns toward the chief producer. "Congratulations, David! You knew you and Leslie would make a wonderful team."

"Indeed," he beams back. He is a kind man but tough. I'm often glad I decided never to write an episode when I'm listening to him yelling at the myriad of writers and editors and actors employed. "But it would be better if I could get this lady to write just one episode," he says, giving me a warm smile that I wish I could return. "Her instincts are wonderful. Her words, well, I've been a big fan for years. But she says she can't. Says there is nothing inside of her."

Susan looks at me, then smiles at the producer. "That's the problem with creativity. It comes and goes of its own accord. Why don't you go talk to the reporters, David? I'll try to get an episode out of her."

"I thought you worked for me, not him," I say as soon as he's out of earshot.

"I do. And you need to write again," Susan says. "Television is a small medium, much like a short story. That's where your roots are, Leslie. You need to return to your center."

"There's nothing there," I say as I start to walk away. I pause as she touches my arm.

"I've made an appointment for you the day after tomorrow. I'll send a car for you," she says. "Just come; I think I know a way to jump-start your creative juices."

She probably does, so I agree to her plan but I'll call tomorrow to find out where she's taking me. Anything would help me now that Frank is out on parole. He hasn't called yet, but the more I'm out the smaller are the chances I'll be in when he calls. I plaster a nice smile on my face as a reporter comes over and the camerawoman takes my picture. Very politely I say I'm very happy, continuing the fantasy just as the actors do.

I double-check the address in my appointment book and look up at the store's sign. *Eros Technology: Making Life a Little Easier*. I roll the name around in my mind until I recognize it. I'm just turning around to leave when Susan spots me from inside the doors and calls out to me. I put a firm, semi-threatening expression on and join her.

"Oh, now don't give me that face," Susan says as though she is comforting a child. "You have the money, and you have desires. You've never tried to make the two work together."

"I don't hire whores or professionals," I remind her.

"Don't worry. The only professionals here you can't take home with you," she replies as she steers me into an elevator.

Instead of going up we head down one floor. As the doors open a gentleman in a dark three-piece suit, his hairline receding, greets us. "Ladies, you must be my ten o'clock. I'm Reginald, one of the sales reps here at Eros Technologies. And I'm informed that you are looking to buy."

"That's right," Susan says immediately.

"No, it is not," I correct.

"She means that we're here to look first," Susan says, giving my arm a yank. "You understand that Ms. Stanwick doesn't want to spend her good money unless you can fulfill her requirements."

"Of course," the sales rep agrees as he turns his smile toward me and motions for us to follow him.

As we walk behind him, Susan quickly tells me to just relax. "You don't have to buy, Leslie. But this is a very difficult place to get a private showing in and I've given you my entire day. Can't you just go along with me and have some fun?" So go along I do. Who knows; maybe this will inspire me to write that episode everyone is hounding me about.

As we sit in two very comfortable leather chairs a screen is dropped down to show us the enchanting world of Eros Technologies. As we watch and listen to the sales pitch, a very attractive man delivers drinks and fresh cubed fruit for us. Susan interrupts at one point and asks if he is one of their androids, then pouts when answered in the negative. Androids are very expensive to design and program, far too valuable to use as display models.

"Then how does one pick one out?" I ask, then realize too late that I have in effect confirmed that I am looking to buy.

"Ah, Madame, you will custom-design your model to your specifications. As you can see from our video, we have a enormous selection of options and a wide range of standard choices," he says as he calls up an inventory.

"I'm not saying that I'm buying," I quickly explain.

"Oh, don't worry; we'll play around with it a bit. The final decision is entirely yours," the sales rep says with a large smile. "Until you've ordered, whatever you design today will just remain on file, for you to change or use later."

Susan turns to me with a grin. "Come on, it sounds like fun. Designing the perfect slave. Does that sound enticing?"

I close my eyes, and a million characters roam across my field of vision. All of them were at one time my ideal, all of them are homeless in my mind as the pain of the past forces me to ignore my desires. "There are no legal obligations?"

The sales rep takes a certificate from the desk and signs it, then hands it to me. "This states so, and I've signed and dated it for you. The legal obligations would be if you decide to order."

"And then what?"

"Then Eros Technologies must have your android ready for pickup on the date specified. You have to pay the balance, by either charge or loan. And we agree to provide free basic maintenance as long as you follow the instruction manual," he says, now handing me such a document. They're using a lot of expensive paper here. These robots must cost a fortune. "Shall we begin?" he asks, looking like a naughty child about to draw up plans to commit some prank on the school principal.

I haven't been creative in months; heck, years. I could use something to get my juices cooking again. In many ways I imagine this will be like designing a character for one of my books. "All right. Let's do this," I agree, earning sighs of approval from both Susan and the sales rep.

After getting my name and address we start on the specifics. I decide on a male form simply because that is what I am used to, and because that is what I truly fantasize about. Height will be near my own, just 1.78 meters. Weight, of course, is the ideal for its height and body build, which I've decided is firm and well-defined without being bulky.

I choose the native coloring, and of course long, straight black hair. On the screen, a three dimensional image is being rotated. Susan nods her head and murmurs that, "If you don't buy, Leslie, you're crazy. I mean, how would I borrow such a beautiful creature from you if you don't have one?" The sales rep reminds her that it is a machine, a fact I am working hard on remembering. To help with that, I make a choice that causes them both to draw their breath in sharply. "Green eyes," I say.

The sales rep blinks and begins to sputter. "Madame, this is the native type; they all come with black hair and black eyes."

I sit back and cross my ankles, looking very much a lady. "I thought you said this could be custom-designed for me?"

"Yes, of course, but..."

"I want green eyes, brilliant green eyes," I reply. "Shocking green eyes."

The sales rep looks at Susan, but she is simply grinning, most likely gloating over the fact that this is indeed helping me relax and helping me return to my more spirited self. On the screen the eye color changes in hue, saturation, and value until I see one that makes me sit forward. There, now, is that fire that I always picture when my vibrator is about to fall from my hands. The fire of pride burning underneath the perfect submissive's soul, kindled by the desire and happiness of the dominant.

I am too damn romantic.

But this is a machine; I can afford to be idealistic. I can make him my ideal. Suddenly I'm looking into a dream world where I don't have to compromise, or feel guilty, or worry. I smile at Susan, and she blinks back before returning what must be a twinkle in my eyes. "Reginald, let's continue. I want the best you can offer, then I want the price."

"Is Madame saying she's interested in buying?" he replies, licking his lips at the thought of his commission, I'm sure.

"I may be. If this can do all that I want it to," I dictate.

Three hours later I'm double checking all the specifics. Chef with learning abilities, skilled masseur, sexy dancer and skilled dance partner specializing in the classical forms, knowledge of all literature and mass-media culture, typing speed of 125 words per minute with instantaneous grammar and spell check, basic self-defense training, and a double-thick hide with feedback response capabilities. That last will make it act like I want during love- or pain-making, I'm assured. I've required that it read my own writing first and place that on its primary memory core. The voice took fifteen minutes to get right, but the sales rep, once it looked like he had me, was happy to send out for lunch so we could continue.

The name also took a while. I wanted something that would help me keep straight the fact that it is a machine, a possession. So, just as an ancient master once named a slave something funny, I named mine Casper, which means white. The only white parts are, of course its teeth and the whites of the eyes. Susan mentioned at that point that it seemed a bit mean, but the sales rep reminded her it couldn't feel embarrassment.

And no feelings means no limits. Which is truly the reality I want. Though something seems to nag me as I look at the contract, I push it aside to sign. I'm paying cash, so I can collect my property in two weeks' time with no added charges. No costs beyond the weekly recharge. Just peaceful control.

Back home, I sit down at my keyboard and start writing. By the end of the week, the script is sitting on David's desk. Two days after that, Susan is on the phone telling me that they love it and negotiating with me over casting while David's on the other line trying to get me to agree to co-direct. When Frank's call interrupts I just hang up on him and return my attention to my agent and producer. I finally agree to meet them for lunch at the studio.

I take along a rough draft of another book I managed to write during those past two years. Susan then starts singing her own praises, reminding me that it was her idea to go to Eros Technologies in the first place. I accept her humble opinion and then convince her to go with me to pick it up at the end of the week.

David is looking at us, but he doesn't ask details. As a science fiction producer, he probably already knows what the place is; as a producer he also knows when not to delve into the personal lives of those who work for you. Instead he compliments me on the script and convinces me to do one more, for next season, of course.

"You seem nervous?" Susan says as I uncross and recross my ankles in the opposite direction for the half-dozenth time. She twirls the spoon for her coffee between her fingers as she says this.

"So do you," I point out.

"No, this is excitement. I mean, even though he isn't going to be mine," she begins.

"It, not he," I reply. For some reason this distinction is very important to me.

"It. Fine. Anyway, it's like a new car. I love new cars," Susan reminds me with a faraway look in her eyes. Since she leases a new one every six months, it is certainly the truth.

We both sit there for a few more minutes until Reginald the sales rep appears from the far door where he disappeared almost half an hour before. He straightens his tie and glances back. "Now that is nervous," I state, pointing toward the man, who is now smiling and hurrying toward us.

"Madame, I must apologize for the delay," Reginald immediately states as he comes to us and motions us to our feet.

"Is there a problem?" Susan says as she steps off the raised waiting area.

"Problem? Oh, no, just a mistake on the records – easily fixed, I assure you," he quickly states. He calls out an order to the curtain now before us, then grins at me. He holds out his hands, and I let him take mine. "Are you ready to meet your personal slave?" he asks with a childish edge to his voice.

Everyone here is far more anxious than I am. I look at Susan, purposely making them both wait a few seconds. "You could sell the rights to show this stuff on television and get high ratings," I think suddenly. I sigh then and smile at them both. "Bring it out."

I'm not really surprised when my purchase comes out stark naked. It makes sense, and this is why I almost always have this happen in my stories. What I'm surprised at is the perfection that is walking toward me. Back straight and yet not ridged, arms swinging just enough to look at ease, head bowed slightly so his eyes never meet mine. Its eyes; I have to remember that. It will be a challenge, I realize, as it stops a few feet from us.

"Please examine him, Madame," Reginald says with a blush rising on his cheeks.

"Whoa," Susan whispers as she follows close behind me.

We circle him, it, once, just looking at it. Susan is repeating the same movements as myself, and I see a blush on her as well. The second time around I trail one fingernail over the surface of the skin, leaving a thin red line that quickly fades to be followed by the one my agent creates. I feel the texture and am amazed by how similar it feels to my own skin. No, even smoother, with absolutely no hair anywhere other than eyelashes, eyebrows, and the long locks running from the head to the shoulder blades.

"Toss your head once," I say. I nod as it complies, sending the locks back before they bounce and settle onto the shoulder blades again. I'm reminded of a beautiful mare I once owned when I was a child. The power I controlled when I rode Ebony is a power I want to feel again. In many ways, it may be true that a horse is a girl's first love, her first dominant conquest.

I stop in front of it and run my palms down the chest. The nipples harden between my fingers. One glance at Susan sends her back a few feet, blushing deeply over her entire face and neck, as she realizes what I plan to do. I pinch the nipples, but there is no response, so I glance at the sales rep with a frown.

"Is something wrong, Madame?"

"I thought you told me it would be fully functional?" I reply, my fingers twisting harder and my eyes searching for a reaction. By now even the most stoic man would be on his toes, a wince on his face.

"Madame, it has been programmed to obey only your commands now. Merely tell it your desires; it will comply if they are within the program you selected," Reginald points out.

I release one of the nipples so I can tilt the head up by the chin. A gasp is my immediate response to the bright light shining at me from the emerald spheres. I look deep into them, and for a moment they seem to reflect some type of emotion, although perhaps it is only registering that I am about to give a command. "I need verbal and physical responses from you at all times. Appropriate ones, of course."

Still, nothing happens when I twist the nipples, and I point this out to the sales rep. The concerned man thumbs through the owner's manual, then brings it to me, his finger on one early paragraph. "Just tell him your name, and he will check the voice print to confirm. Then he will obey. Perhaps I should go get some clothing for it?"

"That sounds like a great idea," Susan replies as she takes his arm. "I'll even help, since I know what Ms. Stanwick prefers."

I wait until they have moved out of sight before trying again. "I'm Leslie Stanwick, the woman who purchased you. Your name is Casper. Hopefully you have been programmed as I wish," I say softly, more to myself than to it, but its eyes flicker a bit. "Do I need to repeat my earlier command?"

"No, Mistress," it simply says.

I step back, my hands dropping to my sides. The voice is musical, just as I picked out, the sound of perfection I imagined for so long. Its rich tones are deep, the words clear, the inflection sincere. "You have a nice voice," I say, then roll my eyes at giving a compliment to a machine.

"Thank you, Mistress."

I step back and grab the nipples again. This time the entire body moves slightly and the face tenses up as I twist them in opposite directions. Using my nails I pull them out away from the chest, and now a groan escapes its throat. The groan becomes a deep growl as I press the nubs into the bones and rub them firmly. The shoulders are tense; the neck is stretched; the throat arched up as almost an offering to me; the arms and fingers are clenched slightly.

A downward glance shows me that the cock is responding as well, so I turn my attention southward. The perfection is here as well. Most often I've found the penis and testes to be odd, to say the least; an addition to the male body after everything else was made and woman was created. I could hear God saying, "Oh, well, now how is he going to help in this reproductive thing?"

But not my creation's cock and balls. The light reddish tint of the skin is uniform everywhere I can see. No hair disturbs the flow of the skin and flesh from well defined abs to narrow hips to strong thighs. I lift the balls and weigh them; they easily fit into one palm. Contrary to many fantasies, I don't find size important down below. Beauty and the ability to do a careful and sensual job are my high standard. And yet as I hold and fondle these parts the cock grows as long as my hand, nails included, and thick enough for my hand to grasp firmly without overlapping.

I stand up, heat rising on my own face, as I hear footsteps approaching. I see Susan and the sales rep coming toward me with a suitcase and a bundle of clothing in their hands. "He's fine, just fine," I assure them as I run my hands through my hair. I'll have a long time to enjoy this, I remind myself.

"I hope you like these and the rest I picked out," Susan says as she shows me the clothing. A pair of faded blue pants, a natural tone shirt with buttons up the front, and a pair of sandals. Obviously no underwear for a machine. I give these to my android. "Put these on, Casper."

"Oh, good. You're using the name. That will help with the bonding," Reginald says as he opens the suitcase briefly, showing me more clothing. "If any of this is not to your liking, just phone and we'll have others delivered."

"How much for these clothes?" I ask as I place the owner's manual in with them.

"Included in the price are three casual and one formal set, Madame," Reginald replies with a wide grin. "I'm glad that Madame approves," he adds with a glance at Casper. I look closely at the sales rep's eyes and realize that's probably lust I'm seeing, not embarrassment.

"Thank you; if anything is wrong, I'll be sure to call," I tell him as I take the suitcase. "Let's go," I say.

At the parking lot I put the suitcase into the back seat and motion for Casper to take the front. "Do you want to be dropped off at your office?" I offer Susan as she glances at my android.

She straightens up, her eyes wide. "Oh, no, I think a walk will do me good," she says as she steps back.

We wave, and then I climb into the front driver's seat. "I think she'll need a cold shower," I say with a chuckle. I look at Casper and he, it, simply smiles. It, it, it, it, it! I shake my own head as I drive out of the garage.

Once on the street I put my sunglasses on and glance at Casper. "Do you need sunglasses? I have an extra pair in the passenger's compartment," I tell him, it.

"I do not require them, Mistress."

Of course not; it's a machine. It can probably fold down tinted lenses or something or else doesn't even see light as I do.

"Thank you, Mistress, for offering," Casper adds.

I blink once, then say, "That's all right. Just thought you might want them, to look cool in."

There is a pause, something I wasn't expecting from a perfectly timed machine. "Mistress, do you want me to wear them?" Casper asks softly.

For a moment I'm tempted to say yes so that no one can possibly look into the car and suspect that next to me is anything but a real live man. Then I remind myself that that is the truth, something I'd best get used to. "No, just stay as you are," I say.

On the way home we stop for a few groceries – well, actually quite a few, it turns out – when Casper tells me that all of my favorite recipes are programmed into him. It uses the word "read" to describe the method of acquisition, and when I point out that having something downloaded and reading something are quite different, it merely agrees.

Once home I show my new piece of hardware around the place. Surprisingly, it comments on how nicely the place is decorated and on my wisdom in choosing a place out of the city. I suppose it is just making polite conversation, but it is unnerving so I order it to just be silent and make an early dinner. As I watch it dice carrots, peel potatoes, and grill a steak, I make decisions about this first night.

My plans are finalized as it kneels by my feet and drinks one of the energy shakes, as they are called, from the case that was delivered last evening when I set the time to pick up my purchase. As the gray odorless liquid disappears down its throat, I wonder what it tastes like. Probably nothing, since there would be little point. Casper confirms this by telling me it doesn't have the words to describe it properly, though he assures me he'll be able to tell if his cooking is good by tasting.

When I ask if it knows what I write and who I am there is almost a hint of color on the cheeks, as though a blush in embarrassment. "Yes, Mistress," Casper says simply. I name a book and one particular character from it, ordering him to behave as perfectly as that fictional man does. Most of my life has been spent on fiction, and I understand that Casper is merely those words in physical form, a character for me to play with, to enjoy.

After eating I order it to do the dishes, then report to my bedroom. I make myself walk slowly there. I go to my black lacquer chest and open it. Nothing. I hit my forehead with the palm of one hand. I've forgotten that I got rid of all my equipment or donated it to charities. Basically I threw out a couple thousand dollars of leather, wood, plastic, rubber and bought one big toy worth ten times as much.

I stand up and look around the room. There was a time, when I was much younger, when my hands and whatever I could find sufficed. Can I be that unsophisticated again? I put my hands on my hips. The feeling of cool leather meets my skin. I unbuckle my belt and feel the texture and breathe in the scent. It is well-worn, very soft from being my favorite; it smells like my perfume mixed with leather. Placing the buckle into the palm of my hand I try a test swing.

"Mistress?" The perfect voice of my big toy informs me it is here.

Without turning I make another practice strike onto my bed. "Take your clothes off, Casper. I'm going to try out that masochistic programming of yours."

The body is perfect; a light sheen of sweat covers it, and the welts where my belt struck are turning a lovely shade of maroon. Even though the skin is unhumanly cool under my fingers, for a moment I could swear it shudders. I step back and toss the belt onto the dressing screen in the corner. I say its name, "Casper," and it looks up, those green eyes brilliant and wide. The movement of its head is all that happens. About now, with a person, there'd be a smile, or a sigh, or a seductive twitch of the body. An expectation for more blows or some type of sexual interaction that I would resent, if not then, later.

I step toward it, and it maintains the same position as I cup the chin in one hand and tilt the head left and right, up and down. As I do this I use my other hand to stroke that long black hair back from the skin where the sweat has plastered it. I frown a bit and repeat an earlier command. "I need verbal responses from you, physical responses, Casper. All the time. Do you understand?"

"Yes, Mistress," it replies. Immediately the skin pulses under my fingers and light moans and sighs issue from its throat as I continue to examine my possession. I know that all this is fake, because it's just a machine, and yet it is timed so perfectly, so naturally almost, that I feel my clit begin to throb again.

I stop, knowing that I have a meeting with Susan early the next morning. "I'm going to bed," I announce softly as I take off my shirt and toss it so it joins my belt on the changing screen. I remove the rest of my clothing slowly, my hips swaying a bit. It just looks straight ahead, and I realize that I'm behaving as I might with a human submissive. I stop the dancing and enjoy the feeling of undressing solely for myself. Likewise I choose a simple sleep shirt and not one of the many black outfits that I once used to keep a partner interested. There's no need. It isn't going anywhere, because it is my android, my property in the truest sense of the word. Over dinner a similar thought was a turn off, but now just thinking that makes me gasp and clutch my thighs as a tiny orgasm rushes through me.

"Mistress?" it asks, kneeling next to me where I've crumpled onto the floor. No unnecessary questions, no silly suggestions, just that one word.

I use it to help myself stand and mumble a thank-you before I realize that I'm doing it again. It's my property, just my possession. I needn't be so concerned with it. "Put the pajama bottoms on," I instruct with a nod of my head toward its suitcase.

Casper stands up in a fluid, perfect manner and goes to the suitcase. Again in one smooth, efficient move it has the white pajamas out and on without a word or a teasing jiggle of its ass.

I look at how well the pale cloth sets off the dark skin, making it seem even redder in the lamp light. "Turn off the light, then kneel here by my bed," I order as I hop under the covers.

The moonlight is now the only light as it streams through the windowpane. I watch, breathless, as Casper comes to the side of the bed and kneels to be within easy reach. The legs are folded neatly under the round ass, the knees spread wide and the ass tilted up just slightly; the arms are held behind the small of the back, hands gripping elbows. The long black hair falls on either side of the rugged face as the head is bowed. Perfect, just as I instructed, just as the diagrams in my books show. It moans lightly as I reach out with one hand and stroke the hair once before retreating under the covers.

The sunlight wakes me before the alarm, so I reach out sleepily to turn it off. The feeling of silky strands makes me jump up, wide awake. I blink several times, sure my eyes are playing tricks on me. I reach out and stroke the long black hair again, but it doesn't move. "Casper?" I ask loudly, suddenly feeling very uncomfortable with its complete lack of response.

The head turns toward me, and the green eyes look innocently at me. "Good morning, Mistress," the rich voice responses.

I tilt my head and watch it closely as I slip into my slippers, which are right by its knees. Usually I find submissives curled up on the floor next to the bed; some may have crawled to the end of the bed, and once one even crawled into bed with me after I fell asleep. I turn and face my machine. "Did you kneel there just like that all night?"

"Yes, Mistress," it replies without moving more than necessary for its eyes to follow me as I walk around the room.

I pause by my mirror and look at myself. With my previous submissives, there would be a pouting look at my messed-up hair by now, if not a comment on my looks, carefully coded in subservient phrases, or an offer for oral sex. It just kneels there, silent and still in its perfect obedience. "How long can you kneel like that?" I ask as I start to brush my hair.

"How long do you want me to kneel here, Mistress?" it replies.

In shock I face it again, a frown on my face at the all-too-human response. "All day, for that smartass remark," I say as I set down my brush.

"Yes, Mistress," it replies, bowing the head again.

It is still there, apparently unmoved, when I step back into my bedroom to get dressed after my shower. And again it is kneeling there motionless when I hop over to grab my purse as I'm rushing out to my car. I pause and look at it, reminding myself of how much money this thing cost me, so I leave with only a slight twinge of guilt. This is purged by the mental reminder that it is just an android, a machine.

"What are you complaining about?" Susan demands as we take a coffee break later that afternoon. "I told you that Eros Technology is the best. Of course, he's just sitting there."

"Kneeling there, and it's an it, not a he," I remind her as I set my coffee cup on the table without a sip.

"Technicalities," Susan responds. "You just have to give him a list of things to do while you're out, and then you'll feel better. He isn't a man; he doesn't need your constant supervision. I should think that would be making you happy." She signals to the waiter, and he hurries over with the coffee pot. "Let's face it; you have to pay the real ones in some way to get what you want."

I shake my head at the waiter, placing my hand over my cup, so he hurries away. "And that's what I don't want anymore. Right?" I halfway ask.

"Right!" Susan confirms. "You are the ruling queen of erotica, Leslie. It's not your fault that all the men of the world who claim to be slaves are just self-centered pigs. It's their mothers' fault, you know," she adds as she sips her coffee.

"Is it?" I ask as I stir my lukewarm coffee with one finger. I'm vaguely listening to her as she flips to the edited revision of my second screenplay for the series. My mind is wandering back to my machine. Oh, a few submissives might kneel there for a good hour after I left. And I'm sure most would hurry back to the position as soon as they heard my car drive up. Casper doesn't have to get up, though; no need for the bathroom or lunch. But will it get bored?

"Leslie?" Susan's voice wakes me out of my speculations. "Leslie, earth to Leslie," she repeats until I mumble an apology. "Damn, we aren't going to get a thing done until you call him, are we?"

"What?" I ask as she pulls me from my seat and hurries me to a nearby phone booth. I watch mutely as she punches in her own calling call numbers and dials the farm.

After a few moments the screen grays and shows the inside of my home office. "Hello, this is the Leslie Stanwick residence," its voice replies.

"Casper?" I hear myself say.

"Yes, Mistress," it replies simply.

After a few moments and a few mimed suggestions from Susan I venture another question. "Why aren't you kneeling by the bed?"

"I am, Mistress," it says.

"I didn't know lying was in your program," I state.

"It is not, Mistress," it says.

"So how are you answering the phone?" I demand.

"My internal computer is linked to your home phone lines, Mistress, as you requested in your order," it reminds me. For a second I'd have sworn there was a bit of cockiness in the voice before realizing that isn't possible.

"Oh, of course; I'm sorry for doubting you," I reply. There is only silence on the other end of the phone. Of course it won't acknowledge my mistake; that wouldn't be polite. "Has anyone else called?" I finally ask.

"Two others, Mistress. Shall I play them back for you?" it offers, again surprising me slightly. How am I supposed to keep the it part straight if it behaves like a him every now and then with these unexpected replies?

"Yes, please do," I instruct. I turn the volume up just enough for Susan to hear. The first message is from John, a publisher who calls at least once a week hoping I'll break my contract with MoonShadow Books and come over to him. Susan rolls her eyes at his very high bid. I tell Casper to delete that message and listen to the second. My stomach tightens as my ex's voice is now played back. He whines, and pleads, then threatens to tell my family if I don't take him back. "Like they haven't figured that out," I whisper to Susan, who chuckles.

After deleting that second unwanted message I ask my property one more question. "Casper, if I told you to leave me and never come back, what would you do?"

Susan notes the pause before the reply as well as I. "I would leave and return to Eros Technology, Mistress."

"I'll be home in a few hours," I say before hanging up the phone. "Tell me that he paused just a moment ago, as though he had to think about what to say," I instruct Susan as I look at the phone.

"He definitely paused," she agrees. "How odd. He sounds almost human. Damn, they do good work," she says as she sits back down at our table.

"Yeah," I say as a nebulous fear tickles the back of my mind. I pick up my purse and take out a pen to write my charge number for my coffee on the bill. "I'll call you tonight," I say as I turn to the entrance of the cafe.

"We have to go over this! They want to start shooting soon!" she yells after me.

I pause. "Are there major plot or character changes?"

"Well, no, but..."

"Then I'll call you tonight," I repeat as I hurry out.

That night goes wonderfully. Casper is waiting by the bed just as I left him. It turns its head when I enter, then resumes the position. Taking this rare opportunity to just do nothing with a submissive I lay down on my stomach on the bed and just gaze at him.

Its face is lean, the bone structure or metal structure beneath it highlighting high cheek bones and setting off his powerful straight nose. The eyes are more oval than my own, a remnant of the Asian ancestry lingering far in the Native American past. The color I've chosen is startling and sexy because of its uniqueness. As I caress the ruddy tan skin it sighs and breathes more deeply, just as I would dream of.

There are no pleas or slowwords murmured as I jerk his head back by the long locks of black hair in a harsh twist. I force the head to the bed so the eyes are looking at me sideways. With my free hand I trace the jawline and the lips. I tap one finger to the center of those full, permanently pouting lips, and they open. Its mouth is moist and warm, eager, as I shove my finger inside and up to the roof.

The green eyes twinkle as I tickle the skin there with my nail. Suddenly my finger is sucked down into the throat, and pleasure shoots up my arm. I pull my finger out, and the mouth opens as the body leans into the bed. No words, though, so I narrow my eyes and offer two fingers just out of reach. "You need to beg for it," I whisper.

Immediately a moan issues forth as the hands move to grasp the bed cover. "Mistress, please fuck my mouth," Casper whimpers, its voice sounds almost horny as it obeys. The tongue begins lapping at the now-reachable fingertips. "Please, Mistress, let your property serve you," it begs again.

I run both fingers around the lips, never close enough for them to enter, just teasingly on the edge. The words now have desperate gasps behind them as the head moves to follow my fingers. When I pull my hand upward, holding it several inches out of reach, the face is turned toward them, the tongue jutting out as the hands twist the bed covers into tight rolls.

"Just lick the tips," I order as I offer all five fingers now. I gasp as the tongue touches each tip and starts to move at an incredible speed. The pace is quick, barely caressing the skin, just as though I were using my vibrator lightly on myself. "Oh, yes. That's wonderful," I hear myself say.

My free hand is fumbling with my blouse and bra, so soon my breasts are free. "Do that here," I order as I lean down, offering each one cupped in one of my palms. The vibrating continues as the mouth now turns its attention to my nipples. Soon the tingling raises goosebumps on my skin and the ache starts in my groin.

"Take all my clothes off me, then bring me to orgasm," I order throatily. Casper's mouth stays glued to my nipple, alternating from one to another as the hands help my out of shoes, hose, skirt and panties. Only when I lean back onto the bed do the lips and tongue trail down my stomach.

The living vibrator teases my thighs and outer lips, the hands gently kneading my breasts. At my order the tongue starts to lick at my clit, sending sparks along my entire body. A good submissive can perform oral sex for an hour or more, though sooner or later they all either beg to use hands and fingers or simply move on after a few orgasms.

Not my machine. I lose count after my seventh orgasm and feel myself floating away, while at the same time I feel as if I am concentrated down in my inflamed mound. Just when I think that another couldn't possible occur, the expert tongue caresses thighs and outer lips again, slowly and then quickly, in a firm, increasing tempo until my hips are pounding and my thighs are slapping against the wet hair.

"Enough," I gasp suddenly after my body begins to hurt in ways that I know mean pain will replace pleasure for me. Immediately the tongue withdraws, but the hands rub my arms and legs gently.

"Has your slave pleased you, Mistress?" Casper asks.

I blink at the ceiling a few times, surprised at the question. I sit up and look over at the alarm clock to find that almost four hours have passed since I got home. I look down to find it still kneeling, the moisture of my body smeared across face, chin, and upper chest. "I'm starving," I say; it just doesn't seem necessary to reply to the question.

No demanding pout or repeated question. My android just smiles and rises to stand. "May I fix you dinner, Mistress?"

"Yes, something very fattening," I suggest. I watch it bow, then hurry from the bedroom.

After a few moments I stretch, then head for the shower. Normally I'd go to the bathroom for a towel to wipe up the mess, but now the thought doesn't enter my mind, except to note that I'm not doing it. There's no one to complain about sleeping in a wet spot, since I'll just use the other side, and he'll remain on the floor.

Later, after a decadent dinner and another beating from my belt to replace the marks that have faded, I decide it should kneel by the bed again. With only words to state its understanding Casper resumes his position.

The rest of the week is spent in various teleconferences between Susan, myself, and various folks from the series on points in my screenplay. There are few changes, so things go smoothly. But on the day shooting begins I decide to go in and make sure nothing is really being changed.

I kiss my android on top of the head before I pick up my purse. Pausing in my bedroom doorway, I feel like dancing. It's still there, kneeling, taking care of my house without having to disobey any command. Damn, this will make folks so jealous when I take it to a club. Its obedience is so complete that my mind doesn't even call up the masculine pronouns anymore.

The day goes perfectly, the cast, crew and director understanding my vision as though it was their own. Susan has convinced my regular publisher to meet MoonShadow's offer, and she's already negotiating a movie deal for one of my novels. The only thing that spoils my day is when the police call to inform me that they have not been able to find Frank after I reported his harassing telephone call. No one has seen him in over a month, they tell me.

The drive home is interrupted by a call from my bank. My first thought when the assistant manager says there is a question about my account is that they are double checking to make sure I really made one single charge for that amount. Instead they report a deposit. "How much?" I repeat as I pull off the side of the road before I loose control. "Forty-five thousand?" I say the numbers out loud. "From where?"

With the information I'm given the fear is forming more clearly in my mind. I call Eros Technologies and ask to speak with the sales rep who sold me Casper. "Reginald? Yes, this is Ms. Leslie Stanwick. Yes, it seems fine. I have a question, however, about my bank account. No, the charge was correct. There was, however, a large deposit from your agency into my savings account. I'm quite serious."

I pull back out into traffic as I continue talking. "Yes, that's the amount. Well, what is it for? That's almost twice what I paid for Casper, so it can't be a refund. I'll be there in a few minutes, so I hope you do find out."

I turn off my phone so I can't be bothered as I drive. My mind keeps returning to Frank. He worked, and still does for all I know, down on Wall Street. What kind of game is he playing with me now? I start to call my lawyer, then set my mouth firmly. I'll deal with this myself. Instead I call Casper and tell him to report any more calls from Frank to the police, briefly telling him that there is a restraint order against that man. My android assures me he will do so. The voice is edged with some odd emotional touch which barely registers in my consciousness.

Once Reginald tells me that it is from a former owner of Casper, kind of a trust fund for a future owner, the wheels start spinning in my mind. To the forefront comes a report on television about implants and how folks will soon be able to link directly into their computers at home and at the office. Then one of the episodes from the series about medical transplants that leave a patient with severe cancer cured of every disease by stripping her of her humanity surfaces in my mind. That poor fictional woman commits suicide when all her friends and family desert her. The fictional news reporter comments at the end of the episode that many people would have loved to have such a life of perfection and eternal life so we must all pity the deceased.

Frank's bank accounts, his insane words, his insane acts start echoing in my mind as well. How far would he go to have me back?

By the time I'm sitting in my driveway looking at my country home, my knuckles are clenched on the steering wheel. A machine wouldn't have to pause. A machine won't ask questions. A machine couldn't have emotional inflection and tones. A supposedly new type of android doesn't have money to put into my account. I look at my phone as I dial the police, then realize he might be monitoring my calls out here just as he can inside.

I get out of my car and make myself walk up to the front door and open it. The front room is empty. I grab one of the fireplace pokers and drop my purse on the couch. "Casper?" I call out.

"Yes, Mistress," is the reply, but I hear no footsteps. He's kneeling there by the bed, his cleverly-disguised face turned toward me. The eyes widen a bit as I place the poker against his throat.

"Frank?" I ask, narrowing my eyes and trying to sound a thousand times braver than I feel at this moment. Frank was always quite strong, and if he has had motorized implants he'll be nearly impossible to overpower. "I know that you aren't an android," I whisper.

The green eyes blink, then a sigh escapes his throat. "I'm sorry I'm not exactly what you asked for, Mistress."

"Don't call me that! I told you to get out of my life, Frank, and I meant it!" I scream. A sound attracts my attention to the door. The poker falls from my hands as the unexpected meets my eyes.

His face is dirty, covered with at least two weeks of beard; I can smell alcohol from this distance. "Ah, gee, see, you had to go and try and replace me with someone else! Someone else named Frank even," my ex says as he steps into the room.

I'm not sure what happens or in what order it happens in. One moment my mind is spinning, confused by what I thought was going on with the nightmare of having the flesh and blood Frank face to face with me. I see the knife briefly and barely register any pain before I'm pushed onto the bed. As I look at the cut on my arm, the blood warm, my mind dizzy, I see a reddish-tan figure slam Frank against the wall and knock the knife onto the floor.

"But I thought..." I say as Casper's emerald eyes meet mine.

"Please be still, Mistress; I've called the police and an ambulance," he says before leaving me. I hear Frank curse and the sound of something hitting the wall again before everything goes black.

When I awaken in the hospital, the first face I see has the most lovely green eyes. I reach up and touch its cheek; the cool temperature is nice to feel. "I'm sorry, Casper. I've been working for television too long," I say.

"Actually, you haven't," says Susan's voice. Her face appears on the other side of me. "He called me," she replies. "He told me what happened, among other things," she adds, looking across me.

I follow her eyes and spot the sales rep from Eros Technology standing next to Casper. "Reginald? What are you doing here?"

"Ms. Stanwick, I must apologize. I had no idea; I swear I had no idea that you were given such a new model," he says quickly.

"Not quite the truth," says another voice, which I recognize as my lawyer's. I can't see him, but I suspect that whatever this is all about is already worked out to a large degree.

"Yes, well, you wanted an android, and you were given, uh," Reginald begins before pausing to he look down, then back up at me. "A cyborg."

"What?" Instead of answering questions, this crowd is only increasing the pain in my head. "What are you talking about?"

Taking what seems like forever, my lawyer, the sales rep, and Casper tell me his story. A man who so desired to be a real slave, yet who was never able to please a woman as completely as he wanted to. Often it was some type of physical limit or sexual overuse that caused him disappointment. Oddly enough, it was he who ended each relationship, because he didn't feel he was truly serving the dominant in a pure way. A list of these former partners is provided for me so that I can check his story, but my lawyer is already having his secretary do that.

Apparently there were no laws dealing with such a situation. The surgery was performed in Europe and a huge fee paid to Eros Technologies, where he had previously worked, under stipulation that he be sold to the first sadistic person looking for a slave. The sex of the new body and of the buyer were unimportant. Casper says he wanted to give all those choices up. Therefore, my lawyer is talking with various members of the higher courts to see if such a purchase would stand a challenge. That is, if I want to keep Casper.

I tell everyone to leave and Casper to go home.

Over the next few days of hospital rest I look over the discs my lawyer sent, both legal opinions and background checks on Casper. His human name was Kurt Mackley, age forty-three, and about as white as one could get. He was a computer administrator at a university, not the world's highest-paying job, but apparently rewarding. Never married, no children, and no significant others in his life. His parents were dead, and there was only one sister, whom he hadn't spoken with in over ten years. In college he had high grades and was a member of several computer clubs.

The last known picture of him shows me a man with slightly graying receding hair and glasses, around thirty pounds overweight. Now I've always said that looks aren't important to me, but looking at this I realize I would never have dated Kurt Mackley. I wonder if I ever saw him, since the records show he was a member of a few of the same clubs and organizations as me. Nothing clicks in my mind. If I did, he didn't make an impression.

Susan stops by each day, often with a gift or two from the series crew, writers, or actors. She also wants to give me her opinion of the entire thing. "It's creepy, isn't it? I mean, it's like a horror story about science gone mad and how depression ruins people's lives."

I pick up the discs. "He was interviewed by a psychologist. No sign of any type of mental illness," I inform her.

"They must have missed it then," she insists as she steps back from the flowers she brought and placed on the stand near the door. "It just doesn't make sense to give up your life like this."

"But folks do it all the time by signing contracts and getting married," I say. After two days in the hospital I'm itching to leave, but the mild head wound means another day at least.

"That's not the same. You can leave those situations all the time. He's lost his body forever," Susan points out. She looks at me, then shakes her head. "You're thinking about keeping him, aren't you?"

"Why not? He's paid for; he signed a contract with Eros Technologies."

"Indeed, and you were never told, would never have been told, most likely, until this happened. Sounds like manipulation to me," Susan says as she picks up her purse. "And that's the last I'll say about it. Get well."

I whisper farewell and look at the flowers, then at my laptop screen. I close my eyes and picture my ideal android again. The skin parts, and underneath are wires and metal. The metal cracks, and blood starts streaming down. It should repulse me, but instead it just makes me sad.

"Ah, Kurt," I address his picture, the old one, "why didn't we meet before? We could have avoided so much pain. Both of us."

I wait until Susan has left and I hear her car drive away before setting my plastic bag of hospital stuff on the floor. I look around the front room and note that everything is exactly as I left it. The kitchen is the same as well. It isn't until I'm standing in the door to my bedroom that I see what I was hoping for.

Kurt/Casper is kneeling by the bed, clothed in his pajama bottoms as he had been after that first night. Susan told me that he had been answering my phone messages and as far as she knew was waiting for me at my place. I did tell him to go home and wait for me.

"Kurt?" I say. There is no movement, no sound from him. "Kurt." Nothing. I fold my arms across my stomach and take a deep breath. "Casper."

The face turns toward me, and the green eyes briefly meet mine before lowering respectfully. "Welcome to your home, Mistress," the perfect voice replies.

I had run through everything I wanted to say, all the questions I wanted to ask, all the points I wanted to make. My mind goes blank now; my only thoughts circles around how pleased I am by his being here. The fact that his body is a machine and only the mind is human, along with a computer to help and enhance, seems to drift into the background.

I sit down on the edge of my bed and reach out to touch his face. His skin is still cooler than any man's, smoother than any newborn's. He trembles a bit as I run my hands through that silky black hair. "I know everything about you, about your past, that is," I begin. "The superficial things, that is. I have two questions for you." The green eyes look up at mine, no glasses separating us, as there would have been in real life if I'd met Kurt Mackley. "First, are you happy?"

"Yes," he replies quickly, but not so fast that it seems desperate. Instead, it sounds like an answer based on long thought and internal reflection.

"Second, do you want to stay with me, or just with anyone who'd treat you like a slave, cyborg?" This is the hardest question for me. Since finding out the truth I have so wanted to just pretend it wasn't true, to just treat him as furniture or as the android he was supposed to be. But the reasons I keep going back to the clubs, joining the organizations, and dating are the same reasons why I had to be convinced to do that android thing. Human beings can give everything, but rarely do. Just how real is Casper?

The green eyes blink once, then meet my eyes in a steady gaze. "I want to stay with you, but," Casper says and there is a tiny pause, "only if it is what you want."

No one ever said that to me before. It is always the fact that they need me or the claim that I really want them but am too afraid to admit it. "Is that some phrase you read in a book?" I ask with a frown of suspicion.

"Yes," he replies, and I'm shocked by the honesty of the answer. "I mean it completely, though."

A thousand warnings should be going off in my head by now, but there is just silence in my mind. My hands trail down his hair to his shoulders, and another shudder goes though him. "It's legal; I mean, my lawyer has checked everything out. You are considered an object now. Eros Technology will just repackage your mind and resell you to someone else."

The green eyes lower themselves a bit; a swallow of fear is visible in his throat. There is no pleading, no begging, no threats, just acceptance.

"Casper," I whisper as my fingers trace his throat and chin. I place one finger directly upon his lips and the breathing increases. There is no movement. Is this a man become a machine or a machine become a man kneeling in front of me? Can I tell anymore? Do I want to? What will the world say when this hits the media? Do I really care?

"Casper, I think it's time you showed your owner just how well you can please her," I suggest.

I moan as my finger is taken into his mouth and sucked. Waves of desire start in my hands and roll down my torso, striking my clit as a second finger is eagerly accepted. Each finger is treated in turn, the other hand raised by his. His tongue flicks each tip, then caresses it deeply as he deep-throats each digit.

Soon my eyes are closed, and I can only picture and feel what is happening. I have slipped to the floor and am being supported against the bed gently. The rich tone of his moans and groans mixes with my own. All focus is on my fingers and hands; he never strays or attempts to touch me anywhere else.

My groin tenses with an old feeling I never thought I'd feel again. The feeling I had during my first years of scening, the feeling of power and control, of pure pleasure without concern for safety or the other person. I pull my fingers free for a moment, and his words make me gasp with the first pulses of an orgasm.

"Use your property, please."

As I twitch and shove my fingers into his mouth, the world spins and floats away. Far away I hear myself screaming but all I can think of is how wonderful I feel.

When I finally open my eyes and look over at the clock on the wall, I see that a good hour has passed. My fingers are still in his mouth, his tongue just working gently, but not seeming like he's tired and hoping I've had enough. No, the attentions are instead intended to hold me at the level of arousal I am currently at. No demands for more, no pleas for less, just being there for me.

I pull my hands away and grip his hair. "Mine," I whisper. The green eyes twinkle. "Mine," I repeat several times. I sigh, and the room spins around, though this time it's from my blood sugar's being low. "The chocolate ice cream is in the freezer," I simply say.

As I sit on the floor watching him rise in one fluid motion then listen to the soft pad of his footsteps, I smile. The room smells like me, my pants are soaked, and I couldn't care less. For the first time, I can say I feel more than human myself.

Since You Asked, I Will Tell You

Why does he call me Savior? This is many years ago, the time you ask me about. Yes, it is these same men you see here each day of your life.

Yes, yes. I will tell you all about it in my own way.

When I first saw him at the inn, I must admit that I wasn't that impressed. Beautiful? Yes, but then most serving-boys are in the finer inns of the big cities. Goddess knows I've seen many pretty faces and many tight asses. If that was all I wanted I could apologize to my mother and return to her estate. Beauty is nice, but it doesn't last.

Yet something about this serving-boy caught my eye. For most women, it would be his lithe form, thin but well proportioned. The few clothes worn by these slaves leave little to the imagination. For others it might be the way his bangs hung lopsided over one eye. True, that light brown silk was a temptation to my hands. Still others would be intrigued by his blue eyes with that wounded-puppy look. But I noticed that he squinted a lot when looking over the customers in the room. Some would be impressed by the way he seemed to glide from table to table, body posed just so in respect to each customer. I know that's a learned skill.

All of these things together did make me want to rent the creature for an hour or two that night. But something made me wait.

After two days of eating in the back where I could observe all, I figured out which tables the aforementioned boy worked. I made sure to sit in his section my third day at the inn.

I watched him closely as he moved to the other tables during breakfast, my eyes roaming over his body when he approached my table. No piercings, no brands, no tattoos were visible to my examination. This likely meant that the innkeeper wasn't looking to own the boy long.

"How may I serve you?"

Heavens! What a lovely voice he had. I ordered just enough to break my fast but held up my hand as he made a move to leave. "Do you have a name?" I asked. Some slaves do; some don't.

"No, Madame," he replied; his eyes looked sad at this admission.

I waved him away. As he hurried to the kitchens with my order, I carefully watched his moves. Maybe an entire evening with him would be relaxing.

Lunch time proved more interesting. I sat a little further back, yet still in his section. After visiting the postal depot and reading another summons from my mother, I was very hungry. The boy took my large order and hurried to fetch it. He didn't even flinch when I pinched his ass. That was disappointing.

The tray he carried my meal back on was finer than any other I'd seen in this inn. This suggested that my mother had not only traced me to this city but had spoken with the innkeeper as well.

We had at this time three big conflicts. First, I like to go out and see how the commoners live; she didn't approve. The second was a lack of a granddaughter after three years' time. The last is what I am speaking about now: my sexual art.

Something was obviously said to the boy as well, for he moved even more gracefully as he set the food on my table.

"Didn't you ever have a name?" I asked him.

"No, Madame," he replied. "You may use my number," he suggested, holding up his left wrist so I could see his ID bracelet, "or call me whatever you wish."

I smiled as I looked him over once more. A few rings here and there and he would be pretty indeed. I waved him away before my mind pushed any other crazy thoughts into my head.

As I finished my lunch, I turned toward the kitchen, from which a loud ruckus could be heard. The door swung back, and the innkeeper pulled my serving-boy after her by the nape of his neck. She steered him to the punishment corner of the room where anyone in the inn could watch. I stood up and went closer to the action.

Every public place has a punishment area. The purpose, other than to provide an area for whippings, is to humiliate the slave as well. Under the gaze of strangers, or in this case customers, a slave received his punishment. The onlookers might well add their own afterwards. For a serving-boy this would likely be no tips for several days. This would further tie him to his current situation, since without money he could never hope to buy a higher position or attract another master.

The boy's hands were tied to the two poles, forcing his body to be an open target. I moved to the side of one of the poles so I could watch his face carefully. He glanced at me and seemed to be flirting as he slowly lowered his head, eyes focused on mine until the last moment.

The innkeeper wasn't skilled with her bullwhip. I doubt she was interested in it as an art form, as I was. No, she cared only about making the boy suffer. Any slave would have been weeping and begging after the whip wrapped around his ribs for a second time.

This serving-boy only gasped loudly. Indeed, he seemed to arch his back toward each blow. This caused me to rethink my plans for the evening. When his gasps turned to moans and his hands clenched at the chains, I had to bite my lower lip to remind myself to stay where I was. My hands seemed so cold, and his skin seemed to be radiating heat. My mind ran an inventory of all the tools I had in my room upstairs as pictures began to form.

Suddenly the innkeeper stopped. She stepped back and nodded to two of her employees. The boy looked over his shoulder as his wrists were unchained. "Please, Master, may I have another?" he whispered.

I stepped back, my mouth hanging open, at his words. The innkeeper only laughed and walked away.

The serving-boy sighed sadly and was led back to the kitchen.

I returned to my table and sat there picking at the remains of a roll until the serving-boy's voice interrupted my thinking. I looked at him, sure it must be another boy, since mine would need time to recover. Yet it was the same boy. He seemed to be a little shaky as he stood there holding the fine tray.

"Would you like anything else?" he asked, his head and eyes doing that flirting thing again.

I pushed myself back from the table and stood up. The boy was several inches taller than me, but his status made him seen so much smaller.

"Anything," he whispered, now that I was close enough to hear.

I turned my head quickly so my long braid flipped over one shoulder and struck his chest. I smiled when he gasped. "Maybe after supper," I teased, then left the inn.

At supper, I sat at the table farthest from the kitchen, yet still in that boy's section. He was clearly shaking as he returned with my food. I placed my hand over his as he set the last plate on the table. "Tell your master that I wish to speak with her," I instructed him softly.

His eyes looked at mine eagerly as he nodded. All grace vanished as he hurried back to the kitchen. Soon he led the innkeeper to my table.

"How may I help you?" she inquired with a smile and a bow I'm sure she only used for aristocrats. Yes, my mother had spoken with her.

"I find the boy intriguing," I said. "How much for him, starting now and ending tomorrow after breakfast?"

The innkeeper blinked once, as did the boy. "Him? This common serving slave?" she asked with a look of disbelief. When I nodded, she spread her hands out humbly. "Please accept his service as a gift."

I frowned then and set my money pouch on the table. "I must insist that you charge me," I told her firmly.

The innkeeper sighed. "For him, a mere copper."

I took the coin and set it in the palm of the innkeeper's hand. She departed, and the boy stayed, his head now bowed. For evening meals the serving slaves here add a vest to the simple shorts they always wear. The dull gray color did little to highlight his features. As though he could read my mind, he seemed to withdraw into himself.

"Sit," I commanded as I tapped the floor with one boot. He sank to the floor and sat cross-legged. His head remained bowed, his shoulders hunched forward, as I ate. After a moment, I took a piece of bread and handed it down to him. He didn't move, so I spoke. "How are you going to see what I need if your head is bowed?"

He looked up from under his bangs at me, then at the bread. He reached for it, but I pulled it away.

"No, I want you to eat from my hands," I told him. "You have been tamed enough for that, haven't you?"

"Yes, Ma'am," he replied. This time he opened his mouth and kept his hands on his lap as I offered him the bread. As soon as he took it into his mouth he bowed his head again. "Thank you, Ma'am," he whispered.

I frowned at his attitude, hoping that the earlier show he'd put on was the truth, or he'd have his butt kicked down those stairs and back into the kitchen before an hour was up. A second later, he raised his head a bit so that he could watch me. It made feeding him a lot easier.

After the meal, I had him lead the way up to my room. I locked the door behind us and stood perfectly still, watching him, as he stood in the middle of the room, his back to me. When he moved, I clicked my tongue. "In this room, you don't move until I tell you to. If you please me, and I spend more time with you, you may earn that privilege."

"Yes, Ma'am," he responded quickly and readjusted his position so it matched his earlier stance.

"Stay there," I told him as I walked past him into the private bath. I tilted the mirror so I could watch him as I changed out of my traveling clothes into my leathers. I'm good, but I'm not stupid. I picked up one of my bags, the heaviest, and lugged it into the bedroom. I felt his eyes watching me as I crossed in front of him and set the bag on top of the bed.

I took out each of my instruments of torture – instruments in the sense of music, the tools of my art. When each was laid out as I wanted, I turned toward the boy. I walked in front of him where he could get a good look at me. He lowered his head as soon as I stopped in front of him. "You can look at me," I told him firmly.

He took my words as an order and looked at me carefully. Now, I know how I look in leather pants, leather vest, leather jacket and leather gloves and boots. Each step is important for the masterpiece to be formed. The shiver that shook his body indicated that he agreed with my assessment.

"Come over here," I ordered as I nodded toward the bed. When he turned, I took the opportunity to grasp the back of his neck. He tensed for a moment, then relaxed and let me guide him to the edge of the bed. "Look at everything and tell me what you think," I said as I released his neck, only to run my hands through his hair. I ran my fingers through those soft locks, then cupped the back of his head. He sighed and bowed his head. "Look at them," I growled into his ear. "Tell me what you're thinking."

The boy sighed again, so I shook his head roughly. "It feels good," he whispered.

"About my collection," I said, steering his eyes back to the bed.

"I don't recognize most of them," he told me.

"You like pain, don't you?" I breathed the question into his ear.

"Yes, Ma'am," he replied. He licked his lips as he glanced at me, flirting with every part of his body he could.

"The bed," I reminded him. "What do you recognize?"

"The bullwhip," he said without hesitation. "Yours looks better," he added with another glance at me. I tightened my hand in his hair and pointed it toward the bed. "The cuffs, the collar, though not one that nice," he replied.

I'm sure he hasn't seen one so well taken care of. I'm very proud of my art, and I take good care of my instruments.

"That's it, Ma'am."

"That's it?" I let go of his hair and sat at the edge of the bed. I looked at my collection. I have a lot of things. I looked at the boy again as he stood exactly as I left him. "But then again, you're hardly common, are you?" My thoughts were spoken out loud.

He flirted again, this time moving his hips just enough to offer himself subtly while his eyes grew wider.

"You're a piece of work," I stated as I stood up again. I walked to the other end of the room. I ignored him for a few minutes until I felt the temperature of the air rise almost in response to his frustration. "You messed up earlier so you would get whipped, didn't you?" I asked suddenly.

His breath stopped and he froze at my question. "Yes, Ma'am," he replied slowly.

I turned around and looked at him. He didn't turn to face me but stood still. "You answered honestly."

"I'm not in the habit of lying, Ma'am," he said with a small hint of pride in his voice.

"Are you in the habit of manipulating your owners and clients?"

He glanced over his shoulder a bit at my question, looking at me under those bangs, then resumed his position.

I grinned as I walked back toward him, this time sitting on the other side of the bed. "All of these can be very painful and even pleasurable, if used properly," I informed him as I touched each of my instruments in turn.

"The innkeeper doesn't know how to use a bullwhip properly." I picked it up and stood. "I do," I simply stated as I let it uncoil to its full length. I pointed with its handle. "Stand in the middle of the room. Take your clothes off, all of them," I ordered him once he was in position.

His skin was covered by a very light pelt of hair and untanned by the sun; there were only three bruises from his earlier beating, an indication of how used he was to such treatment. He'd probably never seen the outdoors unless it was through a window. As I suspected, he was thin, only muscles, not an ounce of fat. He'd be a challenge for my aim. When he slid the shorts down I chuckled a bit at his cock, standing at attention already.

"Getting anxious?" I asked as I slowly approached him.

His face reddened, so he bowed his head and remained mute.

I stopped where I was, just a foot from him. "If you can't answer questions, then I'll just send you back downstairs."

"I'm sorry," he whispered.

His eyes flashed in fear as I grasped his chin and forced him to look into my eyes. "Don't ever try to manipulate me again, slave! I'm not some innkeeper or farmer who will fall for your pathetic tricks!" I tossed his chin to one side, almost knocking him off his feet. I stepped back again and waited until he regained his stance. "Answer the questions."

"Would you repeat them, Ma'am?" he asked, his head bowed to his chest again.

"Do you often manipulate your owner?" I restated the first question he hadn't answered earlier.

The slave shrugged. "I guess I do," he mumbled.

"You guess you do?" I repeated angrily.

"I, it's not a plan of mine, it just happens," he offered weakly.

I looked at him for a moment, then grunted my understanding. I circled around behind him and repeated my second question. "Are you anxious?" I circled again and stopped in front of him.

He looked up at me from under his bangs, his head cocked to one side slightly. "Yes, Ma'am."

I smiled. "For me, or this whip?"

"For you," he whispered and rotated his hips a little.

"Why?"

"You could make me do anything, feel anything, even kill me," he said breathlessly. I moved very close so that his skin was just touching my leathers. Through them I felt his heat; his cock pushed against my leg.

"Would you want that?" I asked, my eyes narrowed.

He looked me straight in the eyes then. "No," he stated simply.

I lifted up my hands and placed the lash of the whip around his neck so it draped down on either side. I let the handle go, and it thudded against his stomach. "Good. I don't want a suicide on my hands."

I stepped back and folded my arms across my chest. I watched him as he looked first at me, then at the whip, inch by inch, as it hung around his neck. His hands were twitching at his sides. "How does it feel?" I teased him.

"Torture," he replied. "I can imagine what it will feel like striking my flesh."

I stepped to him and took the handle in my hand. "No you can't," I told him as I pulled it down sharply.

He doubled over with the pain, almost collapsing onto the floor. The angry red marks were clear on his pale skin.

"This is a very dangerous weapon," I said as I replaced it on the bed. "It's not for you, boy." I heard him cough and straighten up again behind me.

I looked over my tools, one finger tapping my lips, as I considered my strategy. Every general, every ruler, every artist, must have clear goals in mind. An image of my lonely suite back at the estate entered my mind. I picked up my good dagger, the one I kept sharp enough to cut spider's web and clean enough for brain surgery. In another hand I grasped another tool and clipped it to my belt.

The serving-boy's lips quivered as I turned and approached with the dagger unsheathed. I touched him just with the tip on one nipple and slowly traced a thin crimson line to the other, then I trailed it up his chest to his neck. A line formed as I dragged the blade along his jawline to an earlobe. There I saw the scar of an old piercing.

"So how long have you been at this inn?" I inquired softly as I teased the lobe with my dagger.

"Not long, Ma'am; I venture half a year at most," he replied, then sighed as I used my free hand to cup one ass cheek. He groaned as I dug my short but strong nails into the round firm flesh.

"How did you end up here?"

"My master, my former master, lost me in a game of poker," he said, and I sensed definite sadness in his voice.

"You weren't a serving-boy before, were you?" I asked as I moved so I could run the dagger down his back to tap on the top of his crack. He thrust his ass back slightly, bowing his legs a bit, and moaned. "Answer the question."

"No, Ma'am. I was a whore, a very eager whore," he added with a glance back toward me.

My mind spun with hope at his words. There are several former whores on staff at my mother's estate. But she has high standards, and so should I. "A common street trollop, a tavern slut . . . ?"

"Oh, no, Ma'am," he interrupted me. "I worked in the High Brothel in Syn Myloan for seven years before this."

A very good place, though it is in a port city and not the capital. In the ports, though, the styles and the skills would have to be more varied in the physical spheres to accommodate the different merchants and soldiers, but high culture might not be such a priority. Everyone can be taught if the desire or the fear is there as motivation; that is what my mother always said.

I decided to test him further with words. "Surely you receive an ample amount of abuse and use here to satisfy your own desires?" I teased him as the knife now worked its way around to nick his balls. There is hair there, but it is just as pale as the rest on his body.

The serving-boy looked at me, narrowing his eyes as though weighing my words. "A slave is always grateful for any such attention, Ma'am. But," and he stopped until I tilted my head and urged him to continue, "most customers are skilled little more than my master. I prayed for two nights and days that you would be different."

I raised my eyebrows at such forwardness and found my own heart beating faster at the challenge. I traced his longing shaft with the flat of my blade before removing it. "You want me to fuck you, slave? You want it to hurt?"

"Yes, and yes," he replied quickly. He gasped in a half-chuckle as I shoved him toward the bed so that he fell onto both knees with his hands catching the end. His eyes were flashing with lust as I approached, the dagger still in my hand. He licked his lips as I presented it to him. "So long," he whispered before opening up and taking it inside.

The keeper of the High Brothel in Syn Myloan will be receiving a gift from me, I decided as I watched him service my blade. He rose up onto his knees, his entire body arched and active as he licked and sucked the blade. Saliva began to drip from his lips as he took the blade inside deeply and groaned. Not one drop of blood appeared. I moved it, not wishing to simply be entertained by his obvious skill. Oh there were great scenes here for me to create, more than this mere inn could provide me room for.

When I withdrew the dagger he moaned and looked at me, his eyes begging like a forlorn puppy just losing his bone. "Please cut me, Ma'am. Please hurt me, Lady."

I flicked the blade down and broke the skin on his left breast just enough for a thin line of blood to rise and drip once. He gasped and thrust forward with his groin.

"That's not the side I want," I stated as I tossed him face down against the bed. As he hurried into a better position, his legs spread but his ass raised high and opened further by his eager hands, I took the opportunity to switch knives.

The art dictates that mutilation is dangerous when not done for a purpose. The purpose would be ritual, or a permanent mark. There will be time enough for that later, and with such a clean slate of a body, plenty of room.

This dagger was dripping with salve as I pulled it from the sheath. It's a disposable one that I carry with me in hopes of such a find as this slave. The edges are dulled and the blade thicker, so that it provides more feeling with less risk. If the canvas were destroyed, where would I next create my master-pieces?

The serving-boy, no, make that whore, one of the most eager I've ever seen, moaned as I pushed the blade into him up to the hilt. He bowed his head to the bed, laying one cheek on it and trying to see what I was doing in the mirror I'd angled earlier. He gasped as I pushed and pulled it in and out in a slow fashion until he was arching for each thrust and struggling with his muscles when I withdrew.

I laughed, because I soon didn't need to thrust much at all as he leaned back and tried to follow my hand and dagger. "You need to be plugged for a nice long, hard horse ride," I threatened in a whisper as I took his once-pierced lobe between my teeth and bore down until I tasted blood.

"Yes, please, Lady. Please fuck me raw," he pleaded, his voice sounded high and excited. He cried as I pulled the blade out and stood up. He tried to rise to his knees but fell back. The earlier beating had worn him out, for all his eagerness now. "Please don't stop, Ma'am," he asked, moving his body as much as his weak muscles could manage.

"Oh, I've just begun, my dear hungry whore," I said as I tossed that blade into the trash can in a corner of the room. "Lie on your back."

He lay down with a slight moan from the pain still in his back and the ache in his empty asshole. He watched me closely as I took a black suede bag from the leather bag, then crouched next to his chest.

I looked at one of the tiny objects inside. These are something I designed myself once, but had only had the pleasure to utilize once before I met this whore. They are tiny black metal screw clips covered in a safe coating that allows them to be cleaned without fear of corrosion. They heated up in my palm nicely.

My serving-boy screamed when I fastened one to his nearest nipple. His tears, though, were mixed with mumbled thanks and cries to Vaha, the patron god of all whores. I was able to use all twelve clips, and within three strokes of his cock after pulling the last one off he jerked once, crying out and exploding over his chest and my gloved hand. This made up my mind as images flooded my soul, pictures of all the various feelings and reactions I could create.

There was a bit of a disagreement with the innkeeper, or perhaps confusion tinged with fear is a better way to explain it. The disagreement was not between that poor woman and myself, but between my mother and I, between custom and art. The amount was settled easily after I convinced the woman that I could either leave with the boy or take up residence in her inn. Of course, if I'd stayed there I'd have had to send for my aides, my servants, my consort, and there would have been little room for other guests.

The boy presented himself to me outside the inn a few minutes later. He was barefoot and dressed in only cotton pants and a plain common-weave tunic. As she got him, so I now received him. Or so she thought, as she gave him a brief hug and words of warning. The arch of his ass and the bend of his knees told me he had obeyed my earlier instructions.

"Take my hand," I ordered, offering it to him from my place in the saddle. I helped him swing up and settle on the back of the blanket sticking out from under my saddle. For a man to even ride on a horse with one leg on either side is considered obscene by many. These same would be appalled if they knew the reason why he moaned into my shoulder as he settled down and wound his arms around my waist. He easily took my largest travel size, if speed is any indication. It usually is.

It was four days' journey at a good pace to my mother's estate, so I made sure to be leisurely about it, stretching it to seven days. Another week before I had to face her lectures, but, more importantly, another week before beginning the project with Tristan that I had fled from.

Tristan. Even now as I tell you this I cannot think of him without an empty heart. He was and is a good man, for a man, for a princeling. I could never have taken such pleasures in my consort, though, as I have enjoyed these many years with Frayne. Tristan was gentle and aristocratic; the first time I slapped him he opened his mouth in shock, fled from the room and locked himself in his alcove until a promise of a new pair of shoes urged him out. Nor could he handle more than light scratches during the marital act and even blushed, placing his hands over his ears, at the mention that my pleasure demanded something more.

What should I have expected from the youngest of the Queen's six children, her third son at that? Not much, apparently. Clearly, since you are hearing this story, I have done my duty to both him and my mother, but I will not lie to you; I took little pleasure in the marital act.

Yes, I will return now to my tale.

The boy had no name at all for six days of this journey from the inn to my mother's estates. Each day I enjoyed his moaning as the object inside him teased him with each stride of my horse.

I have seen many nobles ride with their pleasure slaves in front of them, naked so that all can see the power she holds between her legs and hands. I consider that to be vulgar, and unworthy of anyone who has aristocratic blood.

The boy rode behind me fully clothed. Only I could hear his gasps and pleas as the ride worked his need to a fever pitch. And it was not simply his ass that caused him such reactions. The rough material of his clothing would scratch any mark I'd created the night before, the bouncing would pull on any weights I had strung prettily between his nipples or balls, and of course his bare feet and exposed calves felt each step of my steed.

Each night when we settled down to camp the course of events would begin in the same way. He would lower his pants reluctantly and remove the phallus from his ass, then pull up his pants and waddle off to the woods to clean it off before returning it to me. Then he would gather wood for a fire while I'd catch whatever was available. He had picked up a few kitchen skills and quickly learned to cook under my directions.

Only after dinner, which he served on his knees and ate only from my hands, would the pattern change. During the day my mind was enticed by the sounds and sights around me, the images in my mind's eye reacting to his movements and groans as well. Each night I would try to recreate something I had seen, heard or felt, or try to recapture any particularly arousing sound he may have made.

I did not always use harsh methods. No, once I simply had him lie down on the grass beside the fire as I covered him with the wildflowers found there. Then I sat back and watched as the insects and animals ventured close to him. His eyes grew wild at the sight of a large bumblebee, and a chuckle rose in his throat when a doe licked at the bottom of his feet. But he never moved or made a sound, and as I watched he sank into the world, becoming one with nature before my eyes. That was the first picture from our work I ever committed to pen and paper; our first creation that I did not want to lose when the time came to sweep the flowers away and clean him off.

The insects did leave their marks. He itched for a few hours until I gave him a salve. He never asked for anything to relieve his feelings; he simply gave in to them. It is a wondrous gift he possesses.

His name? Yes, I did not name him until we were just one day from my mother's estate. He'd traveled on his stomach across my legs for the last few hours. I'd hold the reins in one hand, but alternate hands so that one would either be resting on his upturned ass or tangled in his hair. I tied his wrists and ankles with wet leather before I struggled to get him up. It wasn't much of a struggle, because then he was still mostly skin and bones from the harsh life at the inn. Oh, and he did not have the phallus in place that day, so my hand caressing him only reminded him of how empty he was. He'd comment on it every now and then, swinging up his eyes to meet mine and putting a quiver in his voice as he told me, quite shamelessly, that he needed to be filled and used.

The leather around his wrists and ankles, of course, dried, and was digging into his flesh, though not to tightly, for no loss of limbs was called for; the worst thing that can happen is that the image is ruined by lack of planning and care. Art, it is true, is ten percent inspiration and ninety percent perspiration, a good deal of that spent in planning.

That night I did not untie him, and the evening began differently. I slipped out from under him and slowly lowered him feet-first from my steed. I left him standing there while I took care of my horse and the firewood and found us food and water. It was difficult for him to remain standing there, his feet bound together and his legs numb after a day of riding.

When I finally untied him he swayed but made himself follow me to the fire. I watched him cook the rabbit I'd caught and skinned already, and he would look from it to me, licking his lips and rubbing his wrists. All this he did in silence, but when he brought my bowl of nice plump rabbit pieces to me with a chunk of the fine white bread, now harder, that I'd bought from the inn, he spoke to me as had become his habit.

"Did my lady feel how desperate her slave was as he rode across her lap?"

"Were you desperate?" I teased him, as was my custom, then fed him a bit of the meat. "You didn't thank me for relieving you of the boredom of riding behind me," I pointed out.

Those sharp blue eyes looked at me in wide mock-innocence. "It was never boring for your slave. I apologize if it was boring for my lady."

"Boring is not a word I would use," I reassured him.

We finished eating in silence, and then after placing the cooking items away the boy walked to stand before me. I was sitting on a upright tree stump. In my hand was a wide, short strap of leather doubled over, which I slapped the calf of my boot with once. The snap was clear and bright in the descending darkness of night. Everything grew still as the boy lay down across my lap.

Beating can be used for a variety of reasons. Obviously the most common is punishment, but for some it is quite the opposite. Either way, it is hard work for both parties involved. I slid his pants from him, exposing his bare ass, and let his cock press into my thigh and his stomach.

My left arm I laid over his shoulders, and my right arm I raised high into the air. The swish of the leather strap broke the air, and he jumped, then groaned, as I just barely let it caress his skin. Three more times I repeated this same procedure. I pushed him down as he started to rise to protest.

Ten such teasing promises of pain followed as his pleas increased and he wiggled more and more on my lap. Then I set the strap beside me and this time gave him cause to jump as I brought my bare hand down on one ass cheek. The next smack landed on the other cheek. Twelve of these followed as he jumped and gasped, his cock pressing into my thigh with increasing strength.

I paused so I could put a glove on, and he moaned and squirmed in anticipation. I took the leather strap up again and this time delivered twenty quick slaps to the flesh right over his asshole. His body shook, and his gasps became wordless cries. He almost fled from me when I turned the strap and brought it down right between his cheeks.

"Haven't you been telling me all day how empty you've felt, how desperately this part needed attention, slave?" I asked as I put most of my weight into the arm across his back and forced him back down.

"Yes, my lady," he admitted. He jerked up with the next two strokes. "Please, my lady," he asked when a few seconds of nothing passed by. When I rolled him off me he continued to beg as he scurried into position for the beating to continue. I moved aside and told him to lean against the stump. He didn't need to be told; his hands rushed back to part his ass cheeks wide.

The flesh between his cheeks was red and swollen slightly, and yet it was relaxed, even open; he was as eager a whore as any I'd ever seen before or since. I strapped it one more time, bringing a howl that seemed to come from his very soul. He pleaded as he saw the leather strap go sailing over his head to land on my bags.

He didn't know what was coming but continued pleading for the beating until he felt one finger tease his anal opening. "Yes," he moaned, his ass tilting up invitingly. I could hear the air flee from his mouth when he closed it in surprise. The ring I'd just snapped through the skin behind his balls was completely unexpected.

He sat back, completely silent, as I instructed him by words and by pulling on his hair. He watched as I took two more rings which matched the one below and put these through the tiny nubs of his nipples. I took my glove off and cupped his chin in my hand as I named him my property and no longer just a nameless whore or inn server. I chose a name that was old and rare, one which represented how rare his desire was and how old the creations we made in the human psyche were, regardless of the conventions of the time.

The name was Frayne. And when I had said it, he repeated it three times and then broke down crying. I held him there in my arms for the rest of the night, neither of us sleeping, as he pledged his devotion for me and I mine for him. By pure fate, we had found each other and rescued each other from our dangerously boring lives. Boredom is worse than death for those of us with such artistic drives.

Yes, that is Frayne right there, the same Frayne you have seen every day of your life. No, he is not old in my eyes, though to you I too am ancient. He is simply different. The hair gray and even white in one spot, his frame a bit larger and better padded, his skin tanned now because it is late summer.

It is never the same. Yes, I am still inspired by the day around me. Tire of him? I think not. As each day is different, so is Frayne; as each season changes, so does he, and so do I. Together we find the changes, the differences, and play with them until both are satisfied. That is the difference between art and base abuse, my dear one.

Par Delà Fantaisie

"The key is to submerse yourself in the fantasy." I reread the highlighted sentence in the booklet I was given when the camera crew came to my home. I've won some other things before – toothbrushes, a ticket to a cheap off-off-Broadway show or two, ten dollars off groceries – but never something as wonderful as this. At least it claims to be wonderful and all my colleagues told me the same thing. A year's membership at *L'Association de la Fantaisie* is an expensive prize, a valuable prize, according to all the rumored happenings that everyone claims the best-selling kinky novels are really about.

I never believed any of those rumors. Hell, some were even started by stories I wrote, and I know those are pure imagination. Until now. Now I'm standing with several dozen folks just as oddly dressed as myself and waiting for the auction to kick off the weekend. A real auction, the booklet assured me, not like those in the cheap clubs back on Earth. "These are real slaves, slaves who will do as you bid for the entire weekend or week (depending on your vacation package) once you've bought them," the booklet insists. Somehow the word "real" and the time limits of the vacation package just don't fit together well in my head.

Of course, that is more than half my problem back home, isn't it? I can't do the pro scene because I feel so cheap at the thought of being paid to do something I enjoy, plus I can't imagine that the dom really does what he or she wants with the client. Who's paying whom again? The number of begging subs on the computer and at clubs is overwhelming until you realize most of them just want that pro/client relationship without the cash down payment. The clueless passing themselves off as the experts on the computer say "get involved" to find that right person, "negotiate" to find a compatible match. Yuck! Sounds so vanilla to me that it makes my stomach ache, even here in paradise.

The clothes are the biggest problem for me here, I think. This full skirt and laced-up bodice is nice but hardly what I'd classify as dom attire. Not that I own only leather or rubber, but my worn jeans and knee-high, ass-kicking boots certainly make me feel tougher. But that is the fantasy part again. Here in this "real" world of slaves and owners, you are obeyed for simply being a master, or in my case a mistress. I glance down at my shoes, far too delicate to be called dominant, but at least they aren't those damned pencil-thin heels the clients demand from pro dominants. All my screaming, though, convinced the resort management to let me keep my leather jacket, although I heard some murmurs of "savage Earthling" when they left me in my suite. "Yeah, well the French are from Earth, even if they'd like to forget," I said to the closed door after they exited.

I return the booklet to my inner pocket and pull my jacket closer to me in the chilly air. The seasons mimic those of Earth almost perfectly, so it's winter here now, though more like winter in Rome than Manhattan. I'm sure I'm the only new person here this weekend as I look around at the crowd. Everyone else is chatting with their neighbors or exchanging those polite air kisses as we all wait for the auction to begin. I stamp my feet to keep warm and receive a few withering glances in return. If I'm not the only Earthling here, I'm certainly the only American, I decide. Only the Europeans and the non-Terrans could be this snobbish.

The square where we've all gathered is large. Concrete tiers run down from where I stand near the top of the hill to the focal point down by the river so that each person can have a good view. Down there by the auction block are several benches, all crowded by the most elaborately dressed guests, many with servants already attending them. They must have come earlier and bought them at an auction, since the booklet says nothing about renting out "slaves" by any other means.

One of these wealthy guests looks around himself – I guess sex based entirely on the clothing code that is expected here, since the head is covered in a veil except for the eyes – his gaze reaching back into the highest levels of the crowd. I'd swear that he pauses when his eyes meet mine, and a faint smile tugs at his lips before he quickly turns his head. When he glances back again I meet his eyes and smile in return. As if to break the spell the auctioneer rings a bell and focuses all attention on himself.

When I arrived for the first of my twelve two-and-a-half-day weekends I was credited fifty thousand resort points. Each time I return I'll receive the same additional amount. The purpose is so that everyone starts out on the same footing at the auction. Everything else – food, housing, clothes, personal stuff – is covered in the original cost, or prize in my case. What you get in terms of personal service depends on how well or how poorly you use your resort points at auction. I've already made up my mind not to buy on this first trip; I want to observe and learn, so I can make the best use of my prize.

Of course, I wasn't thinking I would actually win when I bought that lottery ticket at the International Leather Conference in Amsterdam two months ago. I just did it because the proceeds would go to an abuse awareness program. Having been in an abusive situation myself a few years back, I hold that program very close to my heart, even donating two percent of my income from my kinky publications to it.

The auction is a spectacle in itself. Most "slaves" are brought to the block in these tiny boats, their clothing strategically torn and their bodies oiled, and perhaps made up to look either bruised or perfect, depending on the fantasy they want to experience. Or maybe they're employees; that is another possibility explored in a few articles I'd seen about the place.

The star of the day is brought on in an entirely different way. This young woman is chased across the bridge linking the moderately-priced side of the resort, where I'm staying of course, with the wealthier section across the river. The dogs and the guards chase her into the arms of the auctioneer, who makes a big show of talking with the leader of her tormentors. After a moment, this head guard holds up his hands, and the crowd, which had been a-titter with excitement, goes completely silent. I myself stand on tiptoe so I can see and hear as clearly as possible.

"This one is no longer wanted by her master. This is the third time she has run off," he explains with a snap of his whip in her direction.

For a moment I almost see real terror in the girl's eyes. "Damn, this is a good show," I whisper and receive a glare from a woman standing nearest me.

"He isn't asking much for her," the guard continues.

"Who did she belong to?" the auctioneer asks on cue.

"That would be me," one of the elite from the benches says as he stands. He waves a fan in front of his nose as though offended that such a display of his personal problems has come about. "She's good in bed, will bend over with a smile. But she refuses to do the simplest household tasks without a beating," he adds with a spit in her direction.

"The good ones are so hard to find," the auctioneer laments, earning a mutter of agreement from the crowd. "But now, look, I'm sure many of you, especially in the back, could use a good hole or two to relieve all that stress in your lives."

I crinkle up my nose. Sure, I write lines like this in my stories, but to hear such an absurd and degrading clichue spoken out loud as though this is real life is disconcerting. This woman is a great actor, her darting looks around mimicking a frightened animal's perfectly. The bidding rises until the auction-eer rings his bell and signals an end. A man just a few rows in front of me moves through the crowd toward the stairways leading down to the river. The sign overhead reading sixty-three thousand, the winning bid. The auctioneer bids us all a good stay and rings the bell one last time.

I stand as still as I can as the crowd parts around me. Others who have made purchases head down the stairway as well, while others are greeted by servants I hadn't noticed before. It is easy to tell everyone apart here at least. No tops sporting collars as fashion statements here; only the serving class wear these silver links with a metal ring and a short solid band in the front. Attached to those are chains of various sorts, which the owners now gather into their hands. The serving class is also designated by less fabric and the dullest colors. The men wear short pants reaching only to the calf with short jackets over shirts, while the women are dressed in skirts of about half the fullness of my own and reaching only to the knee; jackets over blouses exposing the top halves of their breasts complete the costume.

I watch as the wealthy man who'd caught my eye earlier stands to one side watching slaves handed over to their new owners. Odd, because he hadn't bid all afternoon, and yet he looks disappointed that he isn't taking one home. Not that he is in need of any more. No less than six servants stand ready, and another runs down the stairs past the buyers and motions upward. I turn and see a sedan chair, hung in elegant draperies and held by four slaves, all dressed in nothing but short pants and vests. When I turn back to the river I see the elite man walking up the hill. He glances at me again, lowering his eyes and then letting them look at me once more before he is hurried inside the sedan by the most richly dressed of his servants.

Normally I'd be offended by such an objectifying once-over, but somehow I'm certain that his eyes never really saw more than my face and the toes of my shoes. There was no hint of lust in his eyes. You know the look if you're a woman in the scene, regardless of your role; some men give us all the same look. That's one more big reason why I don't scene often or have a steady partner.

I watch all of the transactions until the last pair – the woman they'd staged the great chase for and her new owner – walks by me. The woman is wonderful; she even mouths "help me" as they pass. I pull the booklet from my jacket pocket and look at it. Time for dinner in my suite. "Sounds relaxing," I tell myself as I head back toward my little cottage near the river, definitely nothing compared to the upscale manors I can see from my windows across the river.

"So what was it like?" Victoria, or Madame Victory as she calls herself in her ads, asks me when I meet her and twenty others for lunch later that week. I meet here with the other chairs of the local bondage and kink organizations I belong to once every two weeks so we can keep things running smoothly. I only joined the board two years back, so I feel a little out of place among the old-timers who have served for over a decade; one even was around when the group marked its centennial almost twenty years ago.

"It was relaxing, very fun," I say as I glance at the menu and then press my order into its keypad before returning it to its place under the tabletop. Same old food, same old crowd, and somehow that is comforting for me.

"Oh, please don't give us any details," Duane says sarcastically as he leans across the table toward me. He's one of the good guys – you know, the male doms who actually don't think all women secretly want to ride on their big dicks and shine their boots in the morning while they balance the master's coffee cup on their backs. If I had ever decided to go that route, I'd have tried for Duane myself, I've thought many times.

This organization has been pretty good about teaching respect for both tops and bottoms regardless of sex; I would only call one man on the board and two of the women "pushy" in that sense. Women can get elected more easily with that superior attitude than men can, but years ago the organization split over these problems. Now the bad ones stay mostly quiet, but you can see in their eyes that secretly they just know you'd rather be on your knees before them.

"And what details would those be?" I ask with a grin.

"Geesh, Kimberly," the president, Susan, says with an overly deep frown, "do we have to make a spot on the schedule for you to share with everyone?" I know she's joking, but it pisses me off nonetheless. She's borderline "bad" in my book, but it's probably just that her personality clashes with mine, since she's never acted dommish around another she didn't own.

"No," I reply, "my monthly erotica workshops are more than sufficient for me." Everyone looks at me as I fall silent. They wait until the waiters scoot up to the table and hand out our orders. Mine's the same as always: grilled chicken omelet with rye toast and honey, warm decaf tea and a side order of cottage fries. Duane clears his throat and nods his head at me. "What do you guys want to know? I'm not going to tell you a bunch of boring stuff."

"How could that place be boring?" Victoria replies. I've classified her with the bad ones, mostly for her fetish clothing that I've never seen her without. "Hell, I figure I still have two years of saving before I can get even one weekend there," she adds. She's the wealthiest of our group by far, owning not only her own studio with six other pro dommes, but also having a line of clothing that was the target of animal rights activists last year. Fools! It only pushed her sales up even higher by giving her all that free publicity.

"So, did you buy someone?" Duane asks in exasperation.

"No, I just watched the auction and relaxed in the cottage suite I had. Food delivered to the place at any time. Weird clothing, though," I add softly.

"Are the auctions like the commercials say? Real beyond your wildest dreams?" Janet, the liaison between the organizations and the retail stores and clubs in the tri-state area, asks, watching me closely as I answer. Her eyes have that twinkle of desire I've seen in other submissives when the resort is the topic of conversation.

"It is certainly elaborate. If those 'slaves' aren't other guests paying for the privilege, they have damn good actors on staff," I say. I don't want to offer more, and Janet simply nods her head and sits back. She'll have questions for me later, I'm sure; she's always looking for ideas to spruce up her own shows at her club. For the admission price, hers are the best I've ever seen. And, of course, she'll be thinking of herself in the place of every "slave" I tell her about.

"Sounds like you didn't utilize your prize very well," Susan says as she picks up her copy of today's schedule for the meeting.

"I have eleven weekends left," I reply before jumping into the day's meeting. "We need a replacement for next month's erotica night," I inform everyone.

"But I sent out the check all ready," Angie, the treasurer, says in real concern.

"Mister Backlick," I read the written copy of the message – the name still sounds funny to me, even after the man won last year's best erotica novella award – "was rushed to the hospital last night. The message was on my machine this morning."

"On your machine?" Susan asks.

"I turn the ringer off when I go to bed," I reply quickly. "Anyway, his manager says she'll return the check when it arrives. But I was hoping some of you might be willing to read that night?" I offer with an encouraging smile. Unfortunately this meets with little support, and I end up planning another night with me reading and then signing autographs. I enjoy it, but really I know that the non-published folks have great stuff too. Wish I could get them to share more of it with each other.

After all the complaints I received for not having any juicier stories to tell about the resort, I've decided to make an attempt to "submerse myself in the fantasy." Though I insisted on keeping my own clothing in my suite, I have worn the complete outfit this time, including this fur coat that makes me feel like a large polar bear. But it is warm, as are the boots they gave me this time. Even the skirts are a blessing, as they bunch around my legs, retaining my heat.

There is snow on the ground this time, so the auction is conducted under canopies with heaters blowing warm air over the crowd. I hear a few people around me mutter how terrible the weather is, so I assume that temperatures this cold are not expected here. The auction starts with the cold in mind, the auctioneer moving the "slaves" on and off boats quickly. I have one hundred thousand points now and told myself before coming that I was going to buy someone. I even arrived early, so I'm just a few tiers above the wealthy benches. I note that one is empty: the one where the veiled man sat last time, surrounded by his servants. Others around me keep whispering and pointing to the empty bench, as do the elite below.

There is nothing that I'm interested in buying. Yet I know I promised myself I would indeed do so. On the edges of my mind I keep thinking the next one will be the one I really really want. I sigh in disappointment, cursing myself as the last slave is escorted off the block.

The auctioneer is about to close up for the day, commenting on how sorry he is for the weather, when a great ruckus is heard from the wealthy section across the river. I smile as the final spectacle of the day begins. A man, dressed in clothes that are torn yet somehow elegant, rides a stallion toward the bridge. Another group of men, all dressed in black, ride after him, one of these shooting the poor beast in the leg and sending both rider and horse to the ground.

The crowd around me is screaming and waving; some of the people have fled into the carriages that await them. My eyes are glued fast to the fleeing man as he staggers to his feet and bolts for the bridge. In the booklet, which I thoroughly read once I was back home, it says that an escaped slave who crosses the bridge must be sold; the former master must bid in order to receive the property back. A very exciting concept, one I wish I had thought of myself.

The man just makes it to the other side of the bridge when his pursuers catch him. The auctioneer's face turns unnaturally white as he tries to pry the "slave's" arms from around his legs. The crowd, too, is silent as the pursuers try to grab the "slave." "The law," he cries out with a voice hoarse from running and fear. My clit twitches as I watch – this is what I want, my body informs me in increasingly powerful pulses.

The auctioneer holds up his hands, and one of his assistants rings the bell several times. "By law, this slave," and he says the word as though it makes him very uncomfortable, but I hear it with a thrill, "must be bought here, where he has sought escape." After a moment of looking around, the auctioneer licks his lips and begins the bidding.

A man rises from one of the wealthy benches. Like the angry men on horseback, he is dressed all in black. "If he demands his meager rights," he begins to speak, and then a roll of laughter that turns my blood cold overcomes him and the other black-clad men. Several of the people around me begin to laugh uneasily. The "slave" looks up over his arm straight into my eyes, causing me to blink in surprise, for his own are somehow familiar to me. The black-clad nobleman claps his hands, and all laughter stops.

The auctioneer raises the cowering "slave" to his shaky feet and orders him to turn around for the audience. "So what will I be bid for this unlikely slave?" the auctioneer asks. Only the nobleman whose laughter chilled me bids. All around me the crowd is silent, looking away.

"Fifty thousand!" I call out, raising my hand to identify myself. The auctioneer, the "slave," and the guests all turn and stare at me. The black-clad nobleman chuckles and ups the bid. "Seventy-five thousand!" I reply, earning a glare this time.

"One hundred, then!" the noble man snorts with a wave of his hand.

The "slave" looks at me imploringly, and I can't look back. That's the amount I have; I have no more. As I turn to head back to my suite, once more alone, a small boy dressed in slave garb presses a note into my hand, whispering for me to read it quickly. The note is written in French, the language of administration here at the resort, but I understand it from two years in college. "One hundred fifty thousand!" I call just before the auctioneer's hand takes his mallet in hand to end the bidding.

The darkly-dressed noble turns his even blacker face toward me. "Outrageous!" He is calmed by those of his class nearest him. "Fine, the Earthling may bid, then but she will not be able to go over this amount. Three hundred thousand!"

"Half a million!" I state as clearly and as calmly as I can. The crowd around me stares, mouths open; I feel as though I'm in one of my novels. Though my hands are sweaty, I force myself to meet the nobleman's eyes as he glares at me. I watch as someone whispers in his ear and receives a clout for his trouble.

The auctioneer swallows and asks for more bids. The crowd is silent, as is the wealthy section. I take a deep breath, time moving amazingly slowly, as the mallet is lifted and then strikes the bell. I've won; I've bought someone.

I'm in a daze as the crowd parts around me, most steering clear of me, though a few press business cards into my hands as I make my way toward the stairs leading down to the river. I hear the shouting long before I can see whose voices are involved. There at the auction block the black-garbed men have surrounded the auctioneer and his assistants. The "slave" is nowhere to be seen until I bump into him at the top of the stairs.

We stand there face to face; he is only slightly taller than myself in his bare feet. His eyes are that grayish-blue color that always strikes me as noble, and his skin is as pale as any I have ever seen. Curls of muddied blond hair fall over his shoulders. I note that his clothing is not quite what I was expecting; his pants are torn but clearly reach to his feet, while the material of his coat and shirt appears costly beneath the stains.

In a strange dance he backs down the stairs with each step I take, our eyes never blinking as we descend. The air around me has lost all chill as his breath, jagged, hot, and moist, hits my face, stirring the fur around my neck. At the bottom he takes a final step and almost trips on air. The black-garbed nobleman screams something in French, and the "slave" falls on his stomach, hands clasped over my boots.

"I've come to collect him," I say to both auctioneer and nobleman, who have fallen silent at his display.

"She does not have this kind of points," the nobleman snaps. "She is new here, only an Earthling," he adds arrogantly, but in English so I can understand.

The auctioneer looks up past us all, so I turn my head. There stands a man in a full robe of scarlet surrounded by a guard of soldiers. The auctioneer points upward, and the nobleman looks at the scarlet robed man, then scowls as he moves away. He pauses beside me and looks down at the "slave". "Your secret desires so displayed are unworthy of anyone but an Earthling. But, she will not be here always, and then I will have you," he adds with a spit onto the "slave's" head.

"Hey!" I start to call out after him, but the auctioneer's hand on my arm restrains me.

"Best hand over your identicard, Mademoiselle," he simply says. I do as he asks, and after a moment's scan he returns it. A snap of his fingers and one of his assistants brings a chain collar and leash to him. He presses the solid metal at the front of the collar onto the computer pad, and the metal glows for a few moments. "Please stand up," he says gently to the "slave". When the man stands he is seething with anger; I hope it is at that demon who spit on him and not me. One bottom with a bad attitude is all I can handle in one lifetime, I'm certain. He lifts his hair and allows the collar to be placed around his neck. In fact, he seems to smile and melt into the metal links as they touch his skin.

The auctioneer attaches the leash next and hands me the leather loop handle. "I don't know whether to say you are most lucky or most unfortunate, Mademoiselle," he says to me.

I look at my newly bought "slave" for a few minutes. "That was wonder-ful," I suddenly say, receiving a confused look. "Oh, yes, out here in public the fantasy must be maintained," I remind myself silently. I take the leash and give it a little flip so he must tilt his head up to avoid its snap against the ring at the collar. "So, do you have a name already?" I ask after a few minutes. He doesn't reply, so I repeat the question in my broken French.

"I understand," he says, his voice soft but rich, a strong accent behind his words. "Philippe," he says and narrows his eyes as though expecting me to react negatively.

"Philippe?" I repeat the word. "Sounds like a perfectly fine name to me. You shall continue to answer to it," I add in my most gracious and superior voice, trying to play my part.

He raises one eyebrow, and my heart stops; I find that so sexy. He bows his head and whispers, "Merci beaucoup, ma Sauveuse."

"You're good," I whisper to myself far more than to him as I turn then and lead us up the stairs to the street. The official is now gone, only a work crew remains to take down the canopies and fold up the benches. Only a few people stop and stare as we pass on the way down the street to the stairway leading to my cottage.

Perhaps he is a new employee or a new guest who wants to play this role. He looks around him as we walk to my cottage and into it as though he has never seen this part of the resort. The door locks automatically behind us, and he glances at it uneasily. He steps back when I step toward him but stops when I softly command him to be still.

As I unclip the leash from his collar I read the metal band. On it in elegant script is written in French my name and his as my possession along with an odd emblem looking a bit like one of those old time crests that they try to sell you as a family symbol in the malls and at ren fairs. The proximity lets me examine his body more closely. He is lean but not skinny; muscle lines his bones. Delicate-looking pale skin betrays the fact that whatever exercise has created his fine body was conducted entirely indoors. There are bruises along his jawline, the kind you'd get from a fight, not from a scene. I swallow and step back from him. He's like many of my stories, and now for the first time I have an opportunity to play savior, as he himself said.

I droop the leash over the door knob and motion with the same hand toward the dying embers of the fireplace. "Put some more logs in; get it going," I order directly, looking at him.

He bows, that eyebrow once more arching up slightly, and heads for the fireplace. As he kneels and places three logs inside, I see the bottom of his feet. The torn flesh there makes me bite my lip in both concern and excitement. When the flames are once more licking the grating, he looks back at me, his eyes lowered respectfully.

"Take my coat, and then return to change my boots for these slippers," I instruct, poking the satin pair by the door that matches the russet color of my skirt. His eye cocks again as he approaches, even though he keeps his head bowed. "Are my commands funny to you?" I ask. My voice holds a hard edge; I don't like my authority threatened in scene by anyone.

His grey eyes flicker up, but the arch doesn't return. "No, ma Sauveuse," he whispers.

"Mistress," I correct as I slip my coat off and hand it to him.

"Maîtresse," he repeats in his accent as he takes the coat. He looks around for a moment and then disappears behind me to hang it on the coat rack by the door. To my surprise he walks past me again and crosses the living room. As I am about to speak he turns back toward me with the footrest in his arms. He brings it to the door and spreads his arms out in a gesture urging me to be seated.

Once I am seated, he kneels and removes each boot slowly. His hands caress them, but not like a fetishist who delights at the texture of the material or the shape of my body beneath it. It is the soles, which are covered in melting snow and dirt, that he pauses to rub into his hands. He sets the boots by the door, then looks at his hands and the satin slippers. After a brief hesitation he wipes his hands on his own pants and then gingerly takes up the slippers.

"Good," I comment, "I was afraid I'd have to punish you already."

Slowly, as though in shock, those grey eyes drift up to my face, then fall quickly as he slips the slippers onto my feet. After finishing he stands up and steps back, his hands resting at his sides, his head bowed.

I stand up then and glide by him to the fire, where I can warm my hands. Over my shoulder I see him move quickly and return the footrest to its former place. He faces my direction but resumes the same position as before. Part of me, the safety freak, is screaming to start talking, start negotiating now, before this goes any further. The booklet was clear, however, that once a scenario is begun it should be continued without interruption, or the fantasy may be spoiled. Both of our fantasies, perhaps.

"Are you cold?" I ask softly, trying not to glance back at him so obviously. He speaks softly, confirming my suspicion but wording it so that he seems untroubled. It is a good part he's playing, but one that could get him sick, and then he'll be of little use to me this weekend or anyone else he serves during his vacation. Or employment. He must be an employee, because no one I have ever known has been so perfectly servile but unfawning out of their own desires.

He only moves his eyes as I circle him, like the victims I often describe in my books, looking at him for several minutes. There is very little more that I can see with his clothing still on, but I know this makes him nervous. I want to reach out and see if that bulge in his pants is truly what it appears to be, but that cautious part of me argues against it for now. "You'll have to be cleaned up and then put into some proper clothing," I say as I unbutton the last surviving button on his jacket.

He follows me obediently to the bathroom and makes no move as I turn the shower on and test the water. I look at him and chuckle. "You have to take off the clothes before you can get into the shower."

He appears to struggle with the jacket as he takes it off. The shirt confuses him for a moment as he unties the lacing and tries to slip it down his shoulders. As I step by him and giggle he sighs. "Please, Maîtresse," he whispers.

I look at him and then laugh out loud, but he makes no move. After a few seconds I realize that he is taking whatever his complex role is very seriously. "Are you telling me that you don't know how to take off your clothes?"

"Yes, Maîtresse," he whispers.

I wait a few seconds, then press him further. "Why? You don't smell or look bad enough to have never had a bath."

"I was not," he begins then pauses and looks at his feet before returning his gaze to mine, "allowed to do so, Maîtresse."

If I could arch just one eye brow, I'd do it now, but since I can't I simply tilt my head to the side and arch both brows. "So were you some pampered sex slave then, condemned never to touch your own body?"

"Pampered is a correct word, Maîtresse," he replies.

He doesn't offer more information, and I guess I should be grateful after all of the supposed subs who have discussed their fantasies in detail and then turned around and ignored my own. Most of these had the gall to tell me I wasn't a good mistress because they didn't get every little thing they wanted. But that was years ago; right now I feel left out of the loop. I decide to play along; I mean, this place is supposed to be professional, right, where fantasy is reality, and real life doesn't give me all the answers up front.

"Well, I'm not touching your clothes; they're filthy. Looks like you were rolled in the mud," I add as I study him a moment more. He doesn't reply. "I guess you were well trained," I mutter more to myself than to him; "you are certainly quiet."

"Merci, Maîtresse," he says in a very light voice that sounds surprised and pleased at the same time.

"I'll show you what to do," I decide out loud. "First, cross your arms down at the edge of your shirt, like this." I demonstrate with my arms but have no intention of removing any of my clothes. "Now grab the ends by your hands, just the shirt, and pull it up over your head. Straighten out your arms now, and it will come right off." After a few shrugs he is bare chested, the shirt lying on the floor. "Can you figure out the pants?"

"Yes, Maîtresse," he says with a slight blush. He pauses until I insist he remove them. When they and his underwear are off, I see the mark on his thigh, the outer edge of the right one. I look at it, placing one hand on his chest as he tries to turn away. The lines are exactly like those on the emblem on the metal plate on his collar, but these are colored in with red, blue, and a silver tint.

I straighten up and double-check his collar, noting that his face is even paler than it had been. "What does it mean?" I ask, my mouth suddenly dry. He looks at me silently, his eyes wide in fear. "Philippe, what does it mean?" I demand.

"Ownership mark, Maîtresse?" he suggests weakly.

"Don't you know?" I press as I gather his clothing up into my arms.

"It has always been there, Maîtresse," he says simply.

Something isn't right; something is nagging at my mind, but I can't quite figure out why I don't believe him. I look at him closely for a few moments before I decide to play it cool. "Hhmmm… Well, you'd best take a shower. You do know how to turn it off?"

"Yes, Maîtresse," he replies after glancing at the shower.

"Good. Get very clean," I suggest firmly. Right now, as I leave the bathroom, my mind would normally be spinning with ideas of how the scene should progress, whether I would take a few pleasures first or begin a beating for some soon-to-be-explained reason. Now, though, my mind spins with questions. I dump the dirty clothing into the fire and watch it flare up in angry response.

The booklet contains the number I want, so soon I'm on the phone with the hotel manager. "Oh, do you know anything about tattoos on the servants?" I quickly ask before the manager hangs up on me and sends the appropriate costumes over. A little snap indicates the manager has shut his mouth abruptly before he slowly asks me to be more specific. "On Philippe's right thigh, the outer part, is a unicorn drawn in silver with blue and red beams of lightning or something coming from it. Does it mean anything to you?"

The manager starts babbling in French, obviously pretending to forget that it isn't quite a dead language back on Earth, but I can only make out a few words like "prince," "problème," and "instament" because they sound exactly like English. After a few moments and some clicking noises the manager's voice returns in English. "Pardon, Mademoiselle. I see on our computer that you were not at an introductory session last month on this. I am so sorry for this oversight," I can sense the disgust this admission causes him by the tightness of his voice. "I am leaving now, so I will come to your suite and answer your questions."

"Will you be bringing some clothes?" I ask.

"Oui, oui," he says and then hangs up.

I look at the phone for a moment, then back at the open bathroom door, from which I hear the sounds of singing – not bad either – are blended with the sounds of running water. "So it's a bit of a mystery, a real intense fantasy, huh," I say to myself, a deep smile settling onto my face. "Oh, they won't be disappointed this time," I predict as I think back to the faces of my cohorts in the Manhattan restaurant.

I look over at the full-length mirror that catches my eye as I glance toward my bedroom. I reach up under the full skirts and undo the two underslips. If I'm going to enjoy this, I need a bit more freedom myself, I decide as I enter the bedroom I might enjoy properly, if everything continues so well.

I'm down to only the outer skirt of russet, the matching vest over an ivory shirt, which is still far too puffy for my tastes, and the satin shoes when the manager rings my doorbell. I've also taken off most of the makeup that is the style here and let down my hair. I must be a sight, because the manager and the man behind him enter with open mouths. "Am I breaking some rule?" I ask with one of those angry pouts all managers hate to see on guests.

"No, you may even wear your leather jacket in here if you wish," he sniffs as he stands aside and ushers his companion in. "Where is your ... purchase?" the manager asks with a glance at this other man.

I look at this unknown person, noting that he is wearing clothing very similar to that of the mysterious man with the guards who spurred the auctioneer to develop a backbone earlier today. "He's finishing his shower," I say, pointing to the bathroom door.

The stranger strides over, and I try to step in his way but find my arm in the manager's grasp. "Please, Mademoiselle," he says not too gently, steering me toward the comfortable chair by the fireplace. He smiles and hands me a parcel and a pair of shoes I've seen on the servants around the resort. "I am unsure how you were overlooked for the introductory session, but here is a video for you to watch and a more complete guide book for our resort."

I take the disc and the book, at least twice as large as the one I received along with my notification that I had won the lottery. "This will explain the tattoo?"

"Ah," the manager sighs as he glances back to the bathroom, as do I, as voices raised in dampened yells reach our ears. Quickly the manager raises his own voice, I suspect to cover up the argument, and continues. "No, it is a new innovation, yes. A symbol of a new type of fantasy, one which I think you will enjoy, yes."

"Because of what I write, or because of the little survey the lottery ticket had on it?" I ask, one eye watching the door and one ear peeled for any words I can understand.

"Oh, I just read the computer information; I don't arrange individual scenarios," he replies as though the mere thought is somehow beneath him.

"So the tattoo is a symbol of what?" I press when he looks directly at the bathroom as the stranger stomps out.

The manager looks at his clipboard and sighs. "The tattoo? Oh, yes, it is simply the mark of his former station, the one he was born into. Another means to identify him. Nothing more. Please," he hurries before I can ask for more information, "look at this, and if you have any questions, our staff will be happy to answer them. Remember," the manager reminds me, "submerse yourself in the fantasy." He gives me one of those fake smiles I hate as he backs up to the door.

"I'm trying," I say with a smile back, which fades as soon as he closes the door behind him.

I set the video and book on the footrest as I stand up. At the bathroom door I pause at the sound of weeping. The slave is kneeling on the bathmat on the floor, his hair falling over his hands and face. "Philippe?" I call, and after a very brief pause he turns and stands in the position he was clearly taught was the basic stance. "Who was that man? What did he want?"

"Uh, my former owner, Maîtresse," he replies. As I am about to repeat the second question, a violent shiver runs through his body, bumps all over his skin.

"Put these on," I say as I hand the parcel and the boots to him. "I hope you can dress yourself properly," I add as I close the door and step out.

I have a few choices now. I can use him for my sexual pleasure, beat him until he breaks and tells me what is going on, or I can treat him as an abused creature who must be tamed again. The last is what most of my creations would do; it is what my heart tells me to do as well. "Maybe I can get him back next month," I tell myself as I turn to the fireplace.

I look back at him as the bathroom doors open and the lights are clicked off. He stands there wearing a cream-colored shirt, dark brown pants and vest, and a jacket laid over one arm, the boots and a pair of socks in the opposite hand. I turn so I can lean back against the brick of the fireplace, my skirts safety pulled away from the fire. "You can hang your jacket over by mine, Philippe." I watch as he silently goes to the rack and hangs it up so it does not touch my own, then sets his boots underneath it. "So why aren't you wearing them?" I ask before he can turn around.

"I was trained that it was improper inside, Maîtresse," he says simply, glancing once over his shoulder to see how I would respond.

"And what type of training was that?" I ask, not moving or allowing any change to my face. Two can play this mystery game.

"Courtly, Maîtresse?" he offers after a moment of thinking.

"Oh, so that is a family crest on your thigh after all, not just an owner-ship thing," I guess and receive a small nod in return. "Well, I begin to understand, then, the reaction your entrance and sale caused today." I look at the watch I've kept hidden under my blouse and then at the sky in the window behind him. "Can you cook?"

He shakes his head, the still-damp curls sticking to one cheek so that he moves to brush it away before stopping himself. "I am ashamed to say no, Maîtresse," he states softly.

"No one I ever have does," I reply with a sigh as I head toward the little kitchen behind the fireplace. "Come along; I'm not going to yell instructions out to you," I add over my shoulder.

He whispers something to himself, and a faint smile makes his eyes sparkle as he hurries after me. His ignorance is amazing in the kitchen, but he never drops those courtly manners. I have to explain what each utensil is, and how to turn on the microwave. He sets the table in a very elegant manner, turning with a grin but still with bowed head; he seems pleased that he can do that at least. I don't have the heart to tell him it's far too elegant for the soup and sandwiches he's heating up.

After about three minutes of him standing off to one side and watching me eat, I sigh and set down my spoon. "Philippe, get yourself some food, please," I finally say.

"Merci, Maîtresse," he says. I hear him behind me as he looks for the appropriate dishes, apparently the simplest ones in the suite, and I turn and watch him ladle soup into the earthenware bowl. He stops and looks directly at me before lowering his eyes and hands, leaving the bowl on the counter top. "Maîtresse?" he asks and flinches a bit.

"You may come and eat it on the floor by my feet, Philippe," I inform him gently as I return to my own food.

"Merci, Maîtresse," he whispers again as he kneels down by my feet, the steaming bowl cradled in one hand and rested on one thigh as he eats slowly. I note that he watches me closely out of the corner of his eye. His back is straight even as he crouches there; he chews with his mouth closed so that annoying sound I hate so much isn't present. I reach down and caress his curls; they feel like silk between my fingers, and he purrs and half closes his eyes. If I wasn't so skeptical, I'd guess he was the happiest he's been in his entire life.

I'm sitting in a tub of bubbles now, watching him as he kneels next to me, his head turned away from me, but his breath shallow. "Philippe," I whisper seductively as I reach out and run a dripping finger across his naked shoulder. He shudders but does not move otherwise. I had him strip only to the waist while he ran my bath and then ordered him to kneel there while I bathed. "Philippe," I say again, his name feels good on my tongue, "how do you feel?" The question is one that has driven many subs from me, their own frustrations and desires too much to bear once laid out on display for my pleasure. But this actor is too good to bolt, and it will be my decision to dismiss him this weekend or even to recall him next month, according to the booklet.

"Maîtresse?" he asks, his eyes closed.

"How do you feel? Do you feel aroused, sexually excited, sad, happy, what?" I pressed softly but firmly, twining one curl into my fingers.

"Maîtresse, please, I am not trained for such," he begins to say, then gasps as I pull the curl roughly.

"You're a human being, even if you don't claim Earth anymore," I hiss as I bob his head up and down by the curl. "That means you feel things. I bought you this afternoon; that means you must do as I say."

He swallows once, slowly. "Fear, Maîtresse," he barely whispers.

His head falls forward as I release the curl. I sit for a moment in silence. That was not the answer I expected, not at all. I haven't even hit him. Pampered, he agreed that was the correct word, then he said he had courtly training. "You, you, weren't expecting to see me nude, were you?" I ask suddenly.

"No, Maîtresse. I never dared imagine," he adds, his eyes still closed.

That meant he wasn't expecting sex? "And sex? Were you expecting that?"

He suddenly bows his head to the floor, mumbling, "no, never, Maîtresse" over and over.

"Philippe, go wait for me by the fire. Have a glass of wine ready for me, and," I add as he stands up, his face turned away from me, "you may put your shirt back on."

"Merci, Maîtresse," he says with a relieved sigh.

After he leaves I sit seething in the tub, the bubbling now annoying rather than amusing. I look at the mirror I had tilted down so I could watch us both and wonder if I have suddenly become ugly. Now, I don't think I'm to die for, but my auburn hair and full but curvy figure have never done anything but attract attention, even if it was the wrong type more often than not. Courtly trained. Perhaps he had been trained so that the mere thought of any type of sexual contact with an owner was considered sacred.

"But he's just an actor, playing a part," I have to say out loud. The tattoo was either real or made of very sturdy inks, since it remained after his shower – I made sure to glance there when I delivered his clothes. It seemed like a lot of work for a salary. *Submerse yourself in the fantasy*. Yes, I was driving away all the fun with my silly questions.

Philippe hadn't even ventured a glance at me when I walked past him wrapped in a towel on my way to the bedroom. Now I was sitting next to him by the fire, occasionally passing a hand along his curls and eliciting a purr from him. A reaction cause by two reasons, I'm certain. First, I put on the green flannel pajamas I brought with me, and these cover me completely when buttoned up to my chin; socks cover my feet. Second, I firmly ordered him to sit, not kneel, next to me. He's far more relaxed now, his hair falling over his face making him look vulnerable and sexy.

He tenses, jerking his head back, eyes closed, whenever my hand ventures to his shoulders. They are stiff, ready to bolt, or perhaps ready for a blow. He doesn't look thin, as most of my fictional victims did, but I'm certain he would get that way if I didn't insist he take care of himself. "Get me another glass of wine, Philippe, and one of water for yourself," I add as he sits up. His eyes linger a bit longer than before on my own before he bows his head and heads for the bottle sitting in ice just inside the kitchen.

He'd picked a very good one, but then I imagine they only allowed the best on the colony. It had been chilled perfectly and allowed to breathe properly. Courtly manners were great, but the longer I finger his hair the more determined I am to get him into my bed. My patience is not nearly as long as my characters', but I will force myself to copy their behavior.

He returns and offers me the goblet in that perfect position that you dream about but never see. I sigh and let my fingers touch his own as I take it. Immediately he retreats and takes the glass of water he set on the side table by the chair without my noticing before returning to kneel next to me.

"Merci, Maîtresse," he says before sipping the water with a determined look on his face. He sighs and arches forward as I pat his head again, his lips frozen on the rim of the glass.

"Are you hungry?" I ask between the tremors his reactions cause in my own body. There seems to be a line of heat that is flowing between my hand and his hair and back again. "You are welcome to eat, if you are," I add when he just shakes his head slightly.

His eyes look at me again, and when I remove my hand and motion with my head toward the kitchen he scurries to his feet, the empty water glass in his hand. He pauses in the doorway and looks back at me, then nods with a faint smile. The kitchen remains dark, so all I see is him moving back and forth between refrigerator, cupboards, and drawers. He returns with a platter laden with bits of food, ranging from chocolates I'd seen earlier but had forgotten about to bits of cheese and fruits that had been pre-cut and sitting in the fridge as though for this moment. He kneels and sets the platter in front of the fire within easy reach of my hands if I lean down onto the pillows he laid there.

"How did you guess I'd be a bit hungry?" I ask as I settle into the cushions and take a dark chocolate.

"I am glad I guessed rightly, Maîtresse," he says, his second full sentence of the day. Still he doesn't move to feed himself, but takes the chocolate from my fingers and offers it directly to my lips.

It's like some harem piece I wrote years ago or that telepathic romance I'd done for easy money. No, it's a million times better. The chocolate tastes rich and bitter at the same time; just as I love it. His skin is soft when my lips meet his fingertips. I pull back and chew on the chocolate, my eyes suddenly letting in way too much light for comfort.

"Maîtresse, I am sorry," he begins to say, but stops when I hold up one hand.

"What exactly did you do for your former master?" I suddenly ask, my hand still up, commanding an answer with the threat that it could soon be a weapon in my voice.

He blushes a bit now, but replies very softly, "I awaited his pleasure."

"His pleasure?" I close my eyes, suddenly dizzy. "You're gay," I say, deflated.

"Maîtresse?" he asks with a slight frown.

"You don't find women, attractive, sexually," I explain slowly.

"I don't?" he repeated, this time without the title attached. We both blink and then look at each other. "I have made an error? I did as he bid," he offers weakly.

"Oh," I say with a giggle that erupts into a chuckle. I calm it by gulping down my wine in a frenzy of foolishness. "I'm so sorry; I think you shouldn't feed me anymore, not right now," I add at his sudden look of fear. "Eat some yourself, please."

He takes only the cheeses and fruit, I note, perhaps thinking the chocolate beyond him, as we sit and watch the flames lick the grating and logs. This isn't working either. Not touching him is more maddening than touching him. Perhaps talking will help, if I don't make a further fool of myself, that is.

"How long were you with this former master?" I ask gently.

"Since I was born, Maîtresse," he replies.

"You weren't wearing the correct costume when you were sold this afternoon," I hear myself say. To ease the ache in my groin, I have apparently decided to attack the one question that has been gnawing at my mind since the manager and that stranger visited. "Were those men chasing you from your master?"

"No, Maîtresse, they were Count Domen's men," he replies, adding a bit of detail that fans my curiosity more.

"Who?" I ask eagerly, my brain hoping that I have read this game correctly.

"The man dressed in black who bid against you, Maîtresse," he says. "An enemy of my ... master, former master," he adds carefully.

"You must be very valuable for an enemy to try and capture you," I comment and hear a muttered "très prècieux" barely pass his lips. "But why were you wearing citizens' clothing?" I repeat.

"Count Domen had captured me earlier when my master sent me out into town. He imprisoned me for several days until I escaped once he left for auction. You saved me, Maîtresse," he states with a deep bow of his body.

I frown. He hasn't answered my question at all, but then perhaps that is part of the game. I pick up a chocolate, a milk one, and press it into his mouth. "Eat this, and then go brush your teeth. We're going to bed soon."

I sit in bed, my arms wrapped around my knees, and look down at the pallet he lies on, sound asleep, by my bed. In the dresser I found several sets of sleep and "sleep" wear for both men and women. I had him put on one of sturdy flannel, similar to the one I'm wearing but of a duller color. At first he was frightened when I told him to take off his clothing, and then when I handed him the pajamas he seemed disappointed. At least, his cock deflated a bit; he's too good to let his face show that. Probably in this scenario, the one I'm not fully in on yet, he was only allowed to sleep by the fire in his clothes, without even a threadbare blanket. That's why he's smiling now like he's in heaven.

Damn! I feel so hot under all these covers. There are two demons battling inside me. One wants to jump on him, take him immediately. The other is like the best of my creations, wanting to make him come to me, begging gratefully after I have won his entire tale from him. I have two full days before I have to be on that transport. I decide to play it out a bit more.

My hands, however, jump between my thighs, reaching underneath my panties, then stroking and grinding until I explode with a soft moan. I lie down as quickly as Philippe sits up. Our eyes meet briefly. "Just a silly nightmare," I lie as the spasms make me bite my lip or else repeat the sounds. "I'm fine. Go back to sleep," I order as he continues to look at me underneath fine eyelashes.

When he has lain down, I pinch one of my nipples, and the pleasure ends immediately. I spent a few months trying to bottom, but only discovered ways to control my own passions and get no satisfaction; not everyone can or should switch. I wonder as I close my eyes if he's laughing at me behind that perfect mask his role dictates.

Surprise is my first reaction when I wake up. Not at the lovely breakfast he has ready for me, because there isn't one, but at the fact that he is still on the pallet, sound asleep. Odd; even the most haphazard wannabe would have scrambled up and brought me a bowl of cereal in an attempt to get more of his own desires fulfilled. And, of course, all my imaginary slaves have internal alarm clocks that make sure they are up, thoroughly cleaned, tidily dressed, and kneeling with their owner's favorite food at the moment her eyes open.

So much for the fantasy even here, I guess.

I pull on a robe and slide into slippers on my way to the door. One look back causes me to smile. It's probably very exhausting to play the battered slave so well. On his face sits a smile, his lips slightly parted. One set of fingers are curled over the top of the blanket, pulling it to his chin. I must reprimand him when he does wake up; I doubt he'd expect any less, and to do less wouldn't be submersing myself in the fantasy.

In the living room I pick up the thicker book and carry it into the kitchen with me. I frown at the microwave as I push the correct buttons. Everything must be in French, huh? Not a strong selling point. I'll make sure to note it on my comment card this time.

"Maîtresse, please pardon." His soft voice speaking and the slight whirl of air around my ankles startle me into spilling a bit of the juice I had been nursing. His hair is tousled, all crushed to one side of his face, and his body trembles as he kneels at my feet.

I lick the juice off my fingers, then clear my throat so he raises his head a bit. "About time you got up. I should have thought they taught you better than this," I add with a half-hearted edge to my voice.

"Maîtresse, no excuse, please," he says, then curses himself in French softly.

I frown, then sigh and turn toward the tiny table. "Honey on my toast, and bring the coffee to me when it's done," I simply state as I sit down with the juice in one hand and the open book in the other. "Oh, and a pen. There should be one in the left hand drawer there," I add as I pull the comment card out.

He finds a pen and brings it to me, offering it on his knees as is proper. "Merci, Maîtresse," he whispers.

"Oh, you're going to be punished, just not before I've eaten," I reply. My heart aches a bit as his head falls and he turns silently back to the microwave and toaster. I'm too damn soft; everyone tells me so.

I allow him to eat some dry toast and coffee while I eat, but I tell him to do so over by the counter. He seems saddened by this turn of events, but at the same time he also seems more comfortable, as though I'm fitting into the proper role myself. That disturbs me, so I grab his pajama collar and pull his face close to mine when I pass him on the way out. "Clean up in here, arrange the bedroom properly, and then present yourself to me. Naked. Bring the hairbrush as well," I add, satisfied when he blushes a deep shade.

I examine him for several moments as he kneels there, head bowed, the hairbrush resting on his palms, which are lifted up toward me. His legs are firmly together so that his privates are hidden between them. I press my own foot between his thighs, forcing them apart with some effort. "Are you refusing me?" I ask.

Slowly his thighs part and his half-erect penis flops into view. He seems confused, his hands trembling and his head turning away, as my slipper lifts his balls and cock teasingly. When I take the hairbrush his hands fall to his sides.

"What did you do wrong this morning, Philippe?" I ask. I always make my partners tell me their mistakes, their desires, their fantasies. Too many bottoms expect a mind reader or are doing this because they think it's bad. I'm not a prophet or a priest; I demand communication. This scenario is no different for me.

"Maîtresse, I did not rise and bring you breakfast?" his statement is more of a question.

"Correct. Didn't you serve your former master his meals?" I ask as I walk behind him. I turn the brush in my hand and run the bristles through his messy blond curls. He squeaks oddly, as though in fear, as I continue. "I asked you a question," I state as I pause, his hair in my fist, the brush at the tips.

"I was required to be present at meals," he says slowly.

"Oh, you were one of many, then, who waited on him?" I ask more lightly as I resume my brushing. His hair is silky; obviously he is playing a role, for a true slave's hair would never be this finely cared for.

"Oui, Maîtresse, one of very many," he says.

"Then you have a lot to learn after all." I stand up again and tap his ass with my foot. "Stand up, then go bend over the back of that chair," I order once he glances back at me.

He rises and assumes the position, his hands gripping the sides of the chair. His ass is tilted forward at a poor angle for my slaps, so I kick his legs a bit apart so he must arch to stand in position. The first slap is harsh, and he gasps loudly. I make sure that my punishments are quite different from my sadistic intimacies, so that there is no confusion. He'll learn that later, but right now I want to be as much his fantasy as he is mine.

After the third stroke his ass is nice and red, hot to my touch, obviously little abused. I touch it with my cool fingers and he straightens as though he's been shot. "I don't like to punish my property," I whisper. "You do understand that I must maintain discipline, don't you?"

"Oui, Maîtresse," he replies with a huskiness to his voice that tells me he is turned on. Not what I want at this point.

Three more harsh whacks and he is panting to maintain his silence. The flesh on his ass is now turning a light purple; the hairbrush is hot to my touch. "You don't have a watch. I wonder how you'll remember to get up on time from now on?" I tease a bit.

He just looks back at me under lowered eyelids, which shut sharply as the next three strokes fall. When I reach between his thighs and find his cock limp he moans, and immediately it stiffens slightly. "Merci, Maîtresse?" he asks, and I know he isn't thanking me this time.

"Also you'll need to be showered. That means thoroughly cleaned, every part of you," I inform him as I use the tip of the brush handle to tease his puckered and angry ass hole. "Every part. If you don't know how to do that, you make sure and ask me. Then dressed for the day. After that you make and serve me breakfast. I'm easy to please; I eat the same thing each morning." I raise the brush and give him his final smack; this one sends him up onto his toes and rips an "Oh" from his throat.

I walk away and into my bedroom. I keep the door open and watch, fascinated by the fact that he stays in position while I get dressed. So many bottoms give up all semblance of the scene when I'm not present. He is something special. I wonder if it's just an act or if he is enjoying this as much as I am.

I return to the living room dressed in one of those resort outfits, but I have my hair brushed back into a ponytail. If I have to play a part, at least I'm going to see what I'm doing so I don't make a complete fool of myself. He shifts his weight slightly as I run one hand up from the small of his back to grab his hair at the base of his neck. "Did you understand everything I said?" I ask as his terrified eyes try to avoid my slightly narrowed ones.

"Oui, Maîtresse," he replies softly. He stands still after I release him.

"So go get cleaned up," I say finally. He frowns and looks down at his feet. "Is there something you need to ask me?"

"No, Maîtresse," he states before bolting for the bedroom. He crosses quickly in front of me, carrying his clothing, as he hurries to the bathroom. He'll find it finely stocked with brushes, creams, soaps, razors, and sterile enema bottles. I wonder if he'll shave, because I didn't order him to. Not that it would matter much; his body has little hair, and what there is is very light, almost as white as his skin.

He's leaning against the shower wall when I enter the bathroom and looks up with a shocked expression. Again I've done something he wasn't quite expecting. He straightens up and watches me under lowered eyes as I approach the translucent curtain.

"So, what did you clean first?" I ask as casually as I can.

He blushes deeply as he says he used the enema first, then the razor. I'm impressed, but I make sure my face doesn't betray how pleased I am. When I inquire whether I bother him being here, he admits that he is embarrassed. "I have not a right," he adds slowly as he moves his hands away from the groin he's been hiding from my sight.

"Did the Count's men hurt you?" I ask as I purposely look slowly up from his cock to his face. His negative reply makes me blink. Somehow that was not the answer I expected. My fantasy is of a slave abused in all ways. Yet, there is something even more appealing in the idea that he might be a virgin.

"And your former master? Did he allow you to be the object of his sexual attentions?" I word the question carefully, as though the crude and direct approach might cause him pain.

"He," Philippe stutters then takes a deep breath, "forced me to share my body with others I had no desire for, Maîtresse."

"Oh, how sad," I lament, feeling the words in my heart as they cross my lips. "So you never had a positive experience? It has been nothing but pain for you?"

"Oui, Maîtresse."

I sit down on the closed toilet and look at him sincerely. "Tell about your life, Philippe. Tell me how much pain you had," I command, my heart pounding in my ears so loud that I fear I won't be able to hear him clearly. I lean toward him and pray he speaks clearly.

His eyes focus beyond me as he speaks, but his voice is clear, steady, as though he has practiced these lines often. "There is no time I do not remember living in pain – not always a physical pain, though I would be beaten for the slightest deviation from my prescribed role – but a pain in my heart. In my soul. I did not know what my heart pained for until I came here and saw the auctions. Then I saw the interactions of slaves and masters on the streets, in shops, in their homes."

I nod. The behavior on this resort is decadent, even by Manhattan standards. Even in the cold months I've been here I've seen at least three bare-bottomed beatings in public and several rapes, one even surely a gang bang. In the few shops I've visited I've seen slaves paraded around in clothing, in harnesses, or nude for the shopowners' and masters' amusement. I can only imagine that the private affairs would make even the most experienced pro back home hot. "Go on," I urge softly.

He moves closer to the curtain, his hands resting on it but his eyes still focused over my head. "I think they wanted me to realize that it was not for me; I could never have such contact. The more I saw the more I ached. I would sneak out and try to find someone to use me thus. That is when Count Domen's men captured me. Then you saved me, Maîtresse," he adds, looking down into my eyes. Slowly he releases the curtain and bows his head as I stand up.

I'm far too wet to just turn around and walk out. I'm probably pushing things way too fast, but like I said, I'm not nearly as patient as my characters. I quickly disrobe and slip into the shower behind him. The water splashes off of him as he steps forward. "Stand still, slave," I say the word finally and he slumps forward with a moan.

I place my arms around him, carefully dragging my nails along his skin as I walk them slowly under his arms to his nipples. "Put your hands on the wall," I whisper into his ear. The water slides into my mouth, the clean taste of it and him sweetly tempting my taste buds. His nipples aren't soft as my fingers work them gently at first, then knead them more firmly. He groans as I pull and twist each in turn and then together, his hips thrusting back blindly.

"You're eager, slave, aren't you? Tell me," I hiss as I twist one nipple in one direction while its mate is turned the opposite.

"Oui, Maîtresse," he replies.

"Tell me," I insist, releasing his nipples and letting my hands slide down to his groin. His cock is rock-hard and warm already, so I skip it and simply run my nails down along the sides of his pelvis, dipping in between his thighs and the flesh separating his asshole from his balls.

"I never, you are wonderful," he replies in broken English mixed with a few words of French. He tells me that his body is electric with feelings he does not recognize and that he is blessed to belong to me. He begs me to use him or to cast him aside, saying that he could die happy now.

I press my knee up against his ass so that his balls are pressed up into his cock and his hole is pressed open against my skin. Heat seeps from him, and the water provides the needed lubricant to enable one finger to slowly twist its way inside him. His muscles are tight, though not from tension; only from disuse. Even the most virginal submissives I've had have been fingering themselves for years or using neon-colored dildos bought at cheap adult stores. They never use the ones that look like cocks; most are terrified of ever appearing gay, even to themselves.

"Did you never touch yourself as you wished to be touched?" I ask as I pull the finger out, then shove it back in, my other hand reaching around him to stroke his cock now.

"No, never, Maîtresse, it was forbidden. Unseemingly for one in my position," he confesses. He leans closer to the walls so that the water now bypasses him and cascades directly down on me.

I feel so sorry for him, though I know it is merely acting. He's good, so good, I think as I grip his cock firmly in my hand. "Shall I bring you to orgasm then, Philippe?" I ask huskily.

His entire body stiffens under mine. "Maîtresse, oh, merci, merci, merci," he mumbles after I stroke him once, confirming my offer to be real. It takes very little time, a total of ten more strokes, to send him exploding over the wall and around my hand. I use my other to squeeze his balls, causing him to spurt a final time with a deep groan. I pull back and take the soap from the shower rack. He leans against the wall silently, deep breaths wracking his body, as I wash up.

"Slave," I say as I step out of the shower. I wait until he is looking at me. "Finish with your shower and report to the bedroom. Don't bother dressing," I add with a smile. I'm not satisfied at all, but I fully intend to be before the sun falls.

I can see that the sun is setting beautifully through the cold windowpane from my viewpoint on the big, comfortable bed. He stacked pillows behind my back after my last orgasm without my even requesting that he do so. Five orgasms. I stretch my legs a bit, sighing from the warm feeling the moisture still dampening my thighs creates. I scratch my head and giggle at how messed up my hair has become in my hours of pleasure.

He did not need much training in the oral skills an excellent slave must have. When I pressed him for an answer as to where he got such skills, he blushed and admitted he'd stolen them from slave girls. They had been eager to just lay back and critique his ability, offering suggestions. I'll have to write a good story with a supporting female slave, then, to pay those ladies back.

I look back at the doorway as he returns with the dinner tray I sent him for. In the low light of the setting sun, his pale form seems to glow a bit, the sweat his attentions caused catching the rays as they bend desperately over the horizon. "Turn on the light, Philippe," I say softly. He balances the tray on one hip and one arm as he flips the switch.

I can't look at him as he places the tray over my lap, but the electric light causes flashes of color around his hands and the tray. After a moment my eyes focus, and I can see his face, still damp with my liquid. I take one of the napkins and start to wipe off his face. "Now we both need to eat," I scold lightly as he turns his head and starts to seductively suck one of my fingers.

He sighs, murmurs his obedience and kneels next to the bed. The tray is filled with bite-size pieces of fruit, veggies, bread, cheese, and chocolates again. I glance at the bedside table, and he bolts for the door. In a moment he returns with a goblet and the rest of the bottle of wine we'd had the night before.

"Are you sure you know me so well so quickly?" I ask, making my voice a little darker than I truly feel. His grey eyes widen, and he makes to prostrate himself until I chuckle. "I'm fine with this, for now. Just don't think you have me all figured out," I caution.

"Oui, Maîtresse," he humbly says as he pours a goblet full of the wine. He kneels back in position, the goblet balanced on his palms, which are offered within easy reach of me.

After a few bites myself I begin feeding him about every other piece. His lips and tongue caressing my fingers are like a prayer of thanks to me. Those grey eyes never directly meet mine, though they roll up and half close as though in ecstasy as the food passes his lips. His reactions seem perfect; this is truly a first class performer I've chosen. The wine never spills, though he jerks a few times as I graze the top of his mouth or his tongue with my nails.

I take the goblet from him, but his hands stay in position. Moving closer, I whisper for him to remain completely still. "Cup your hands tightly," I order. He makes them as close as possible and watches me closely under his eyelashes as I pour a good amount of the wine into them. After I set the goblet on the table I poise myself over his hands. He moans as I dip my head and lap up the alcohol from the flesh bowl, making sure to flick his skin often.

I can feel my eyes sparkling as I lick the last drop from his hands and sit back. His eyes are staring at his hands, but it's his hard red cock that draws my attention. I pick up the wine again, then lie down on my back. I pour just enough wine to fill my belly button. "Are you thirsty?" I ask huskily.

My skin tingles as he slides up onto the bed and laps up my offering. When he pauses after taking all the wine and lays his head gently down on my stomach, facing toward me, his curls tickling my thighs lightly, I sigh. "Magnifique," he whispers softly as his hands rest by my sides, not touching a part of me. "Maîtresse, s'il vous plaît?" he says.

I see that desire in his eyes that I have seen so very rarely. Before, always before, I've allowed the submissive begging the privilege to continue their sexual attentions. Always they ended up thinking it was their right. "My fantasy, my fantasy," I repeat silently. "Get off the bed, slave," I make myself say the words, clenching my heart tightly as he whimpers but scurries off the bed to kneel by it again.

"My fantasy," I say out loud now as I tilt his head up with my hand cupped under his chin. "And you?" I let the question hang in the air for a moment as he looks blankly at me. "Is this at all what you wished for all those years?" I explain further.

"Oui, Maîtresse, more as well," he says in the most sincere voice I've ever heard.

I close my eyes for a moment as I release him and sit back. "Put the food away and then return to the floor to sleep," I instruct as I move the pillows, tossing one into his arms. As I lie down he moves to do as I order as quietly as he can, flipping off the lights as he leaves. My eyes do not close, though, until I hear him return and lie down next to the bed.

"This is getting rather annoying," the thought repeats in my head as another guest stares openly at Philippe while I wait for the sales clerk to get my order. Awakening early on my final full day, I decided to use all those resort points I'd been given in some shopping spree. I made a list while Philippe was in the shower, making sure to have all the board members, my mother, my editor and publisher, and the one sister I'm still talking to down on my list.

Each store has been the same experience. The staff stands back and stares for a few minutes until the manager hurries forward and asks how they may help. Then a crowd of guests gathers both inside and outside the store. I'd swear a few of these people have followed us all afternoon. "What are you looking at?" I suddenly yell, causing everyone to jump.

"Adieu!" Philippe says rather forcefully as he steps between me and the staring eyes. Although he is holding onto the packages he apparently can still look dangerous enough to send the crowd flying out the doors. When he turns to me, however, he is all lowered eyes and bowed head, his voice soft and servile. "Pardon, Maîtresse."

"No, thank you, Philippe," I say as I lay a hand gently on his ass as a means to express how much he has pleased me. I have not forgot his statements from the day before, but the crowds had ruined half the morning. I move my hand roughly over the solid mounds, dipping my fingers down the space between his legs so he has to bend his thighs outward a bit. "I'll have to reward you, I guess, for coming to my rescue."

I remove my hand and go to pay the cashier with my resort account number. Philippe's eyes are looking at me, and I can almost feel the heat from his embarrassment and need. Ignoring it pointedly, I place this package on top of the others in his hands.

I don't molest him until we're at the final store I intend to shop in. This one is a clothing store with a selection of costumes for the servile class. I pick out several outfits and then have him set the packages down at my feet before trotting off to try the stuff on. "I could use your opinion," I say to the saleslady when she starts to walk away. She looks at her boss and then smiles and accepts my invitation to stand next to me.

Philippe parades shyly in and out of the changing rooms in the different sets of clothing I've chosen for him. Most are simply variations of the simple garb worn by all male slaves here at the resort, varying in color and fabric only. Then finally he tries on the first of the three sets of lingerie I've picked out.

"Stay right there," I say when he turns toward the changing room after one second in view wearing this obscene first attempt. It is white, its color only emphasizing how pale he is. I walk to him. He stands still so he is sideways to the saleswoman and myself. I turn his face toward the saleswoman and point to his half-erect cock sticking out the of hole placed there. The trunks are amusing in that there is not only a hole for his cock, but also one below for his balls to dangle through and an open section in back right over his puckered rosy asshole.

The saleswoman blushes but doesn't turn away as I gently squeeze his balls and his cock grows. "Do you think this is how all those other slaves you saw in public felt?" I whisper into his ear as my other hand tickles his asshole. He opens his mouth but can only let out a tiny gasp. Suddenly I release him and smack him once, right over his asshole. "Next outfit," I order, returning without another word or look to my place by the saleslady.

The next selection is a navy blue thing that somewhat resembles an old fashioned bathing suit. It is one piece, with straps running over his shoulders and around both thighs at their midpoints. The fabric, however, is open over the nipples and once more at the genitals, as was the previous one. The thrill here is the illusion that the body is covered when it actually displays it more.

The saleslady slowly follows me as I lead her to him. "What's wrong?" I ask, bewildered. "You see things like this every day. True, he is fine looking, but so are many of the sub class here." I direct the saleslady's trembling hand to one of his nipples, urging her to caress it. She moans oddly while Philippe bows his head and thanks us both in mumbled gasping words.

I send him back for the final outfit and dismiss the saleslady with a polite thank you, asking her to ring everything up. I smile when Philippe returns.

This outfit is much more my style. A dark green string ties two flaps of matching fabric, one in front and one behind, around his hips. The flaps fall to mid-thigh and then quickly slope up to join at the hips so that only his genitals are covered.

"Display yourself, slave," I say in a calm voice. My heart is pounding as he kneels and spreads his thighs, lifting the front flap up with one hand while the other rests behind his neck. He offers his throat by raising his chin high, his eyes closed in surrender. His muscles ripple in this position, and his straight cock bounces slightly with his jagged breaths. I can feel my clit twitch as he sits there and offers himself to everyone's eyes.

But he isn't for everyone, not on this trip at least. "Put on your regular clothing, and deliver those to the saleslady," I order, forcing my eyes to look away from him or else go on soaking in his beauty forever.

"Is this anything like you imagined?" I ask softly in his ear as I lean into him when he's gathering up all the packages again. He nods but doesn't reply verbally. My hand between his thighs knows the answer.

He is my pagan love slave tonight, sitting there in that green loincloth holding the tray of food for me as I sit by the fire he built earlier. I'd used him for three more orgasms after returning from the shopping, demanding them before we even left the living room. Right now I'm just relaxing and enjoying his looks and his grace.

The fire dances in his grey eyes. I had to order him to look up so I could appreciate that view. He still glances down every now and then, but I'm far too happy to bitch about such things. Next month, though, I'll demand the perfection I sense in him. At the moment the shudder that runs through him as I stroke his thighs is near enough.

Sitting up, I take the last chocolate and bite it in half. He opens his mouth eagerly, sucking on my fingers as I share it with him. I moan, a new fire kindled in my belly as he impales himself on two fingers, his tongue lapping around them. I can feel the chocolate melt, and somehow my fingers feel liquid as they become part of him.

The tray is easily pushed aside by one hand. He knows what I want. Smoothly he swings his legs under him and aids me on top of his legs. The robe he bought me is discarded quickly, as is the loincloth. While he makes no advance of his own, he quickly follows my instructions, both verbal and physical. Like a wave rushing over me I am swept into his arms, the dampness between my legs making the fit quick and gentle.

I rarely, very rarely, ever engage in such vanilla-like intercourse with a submissive, and even less so with those who simply wanted the physically masochistic side. It was too much like equality for me, blurring the lines of scene and romance to the point where I've been burned so many times that numbers cannot quantify the wounds.

Now, in my arms, in my groin, though, I feel truly powerful as I possess him completely. He arches up toward me as I lean forward, making it easier for me to slip my hands around him. He groans into my mouth as my tongue enters his and my nails rip sharply down his back. He supports me as the contractions begin and my body shakes and jerks as I ride hard.

Philippe does not come but simply nuzzles my neck as the jolts of pleasure subside. "Maîtresse," he whispers but does not ask for permission to feel his own explosion. He hasn't asked for that once; in fact, last night he cried after coming over my fingers and confessed he had cried in the shower earlier. Yet he did not lose interest in me or slacken in following our stated roles. Indeed, if anything he seemed more eager to please me.

"You are wonderful, my slave, my sexy pagan god forced to serve me," I say, revealing my internal fantasy.

He moans and flicks his tongue across my shoulder where his head lies. He releases me with a whimper as I disengage myself from him and stand up.

It takes me a few seconds to get my balance. The air is suddenly very chilly, and I sigh as he rises and puts my robe around me. "I am going to miss you, Philippe, but I will book you for next month, if that's all right with you," I add with a warm smile.

His face slowly loses its color, and he steps back a bit. "Maîtresse? You are leaving?"

I chuckle. "Can we break from the game for just a moment? I mean, just a tiny moment. You've done your job wonderfully, more than I was hoping for in fact, but I really need to hear that it would please you to be mine again next month." I hold out my hand to him with a tense smile. Now I've done it; I've broken the rules, and I shan't see him again.

He bows his head, causing the sweat-dampened blond curls to tumble in front of him. I step back and a cry like a dying animal comes from him as he prostrates himself at my feet. "Maîtresse, do not leave me here; take me with you or stay," he says. "I will die without you, ma Sauveuse!" he declares.

This is flattery to the extreme, and as ashamed as I am about it, I'm wet again just from the idea that it could be true. Of course, it's just a game, but the trick is to "submerse yourself in the fantasy," so I answer as one of my most noble characters might.

"Stop crying, Philippe. Now, you need not concern yourself with the future. I will take care of everything. No need for you to worry anymore about where you shall sleep, whom you'll sleep with, or when your next meal is coming." I help him to his knees, then tilt his face up by his chin. "I am your sun and your moon, your day and your night, your life and your death. With your surrender to me, you lost all such foolish fears as you now express them."

"Maîtresse, forgive me," he whispers and covers my hands with his hair as he bows over them.

"Mention it not again, and you are forgiven, my slave." I pull him up to his feet. "Now take me to bed," I order.

All is right again as he carries me gently into the bedroom and lays me down. He kneels by the bed and tucks the covers around me. Suddenly he is singing a song that sounds like a French lullaby. I close my eyes and reflect on the wonderful weekend I've had.

My last few hours at the resort are spent packing up all the things I've bought, getting dressed in my regular clothes, and dealing with Philippe. Luckily my bags are the type that expand a bit, and I packed an extra one just in case I bought something. Wait until the gossip crowd hears about the flood of money I had. They'll all be giggling with thanks when I give them gifts, then green with envy at the picture of Philippe. I took it this morning right after his shower so they could see him in all his glory and so I wouldn't forget. Not that that is too likely to happen.

I feel so much better in my woolen leggings, shirt and sweater, my boots and my leather jacket. My body responds to the familiar sensations, and I can almost imagine the smell of Manhattan on a grey morning as I finish my coffee. Of course I'll get a few stares as I walk to the main office to catch the shuttle to my ship. I just wasn't expecting the looks I'm getting from him.

Philippe has not pleaded for me to stay since the scene last night. At least, not in words. Instead he has followed me around the suite, his eyes downcast and rimmed with tears whenever I look at him. It was sweet this morning, but now as I'm dragging my last bag to the door I'm annoyed.

"Look, I left you a great tip by the bed. I'll see you next month, unless you don't want that." No answer except his glancing away, his arms hugging his stomach tightly. "Just let the manager know, or whoever is your supervisor, OK? Thank you for a lovely time."

I stop as his hand takes my elbow. "Don't make this any harder," I whisper. He releases me and backs up. He just nods as I say good-bye one final time.

Damn! It's cold out here. The snow whistles around my boots as I lug my baggage through the streets. What is with everyone in this place? As I walk I'd swear that folks are stopping and talking to each other, pointing at me. Geesh people, get a life! I was here last month too. You can't all be clueless first-timers.

Luckily it is so cold and the bags are so heavy that my mind isn't registering any French, so I can't be too offended, just slightly pissed at being the center of attention. After I'm inside the main office I check all but one of my bags with the doorman and breathe in the warm air. I'll need my French skills now just to make sure things go smoothly.

The clerk at the front desk is the same one who delivered the manual the other day, so he speaks in perfect English and gives me a tolerant smile. His eyes betray something else. Not shock or disgust about my clothes, more like surprise. "Mademoiselle, is there a problem with your suite?"

"No, I'm just here to check out; I have a flight to catch," I say as I hand him my passport and resort ID. He frowns a bit as he presses the computer keys, then shakes his head. "What's wrong?"

"Mademoiselle, you are not scheduled to leave today," he says.
"What?"

"You are not on the shuttle to Earth," he states simply.

"Oh, maybe its just an error; can you schedule me for the earliest flight possible?" I ask. This is a bit inconvenient, but it's not like I have a regular job to get back to, and my next book is ahead by about three weeks. "I'll just stay here and leave tomorrow," I'm telling myself when the clerk shakes his head again.

"Mademoiselle, it is not accepting your passport number," the clerk states.

"That's not possible!" I take out my copy of the winning lottery ticket. "I won this vacation, and I'm taking it in monthly installments," I inform him.

"That was true, Mademoiselle, but it seems you must stay here for now," the clerk says. He motions to a bellhop and takes my arm so I have to watch my baggage being taken out the main office. "We are just returning them to your suite."

"Look, if this is a joke, it isn't funny. If the rules of the lottery have changed, then I want to talk to someone in charge. I have a life; I can't just stay here." I'm on the verge of yelling and causing a very un-French-like commotion.

"Mademoiselle, all will be explained to you soon. Please, just return to your suite," he implores me.

"This has something to do with Philippe, doesn't it?" I ask but receive only a shrug in reply. I bite back my comments and storm out the main office.

The snow is just a small nuisance compared to the speed at which I'm stomping my way through the streets. These people are still talking about me; of this I'm now certain. "What are you staring at?" I demand at one corner of a couple and their servants in tow. It's like I'm in a bad conspiracy movie and I'm playing the role of the stupid American to the tee. Well, that stops right now.

He's standing almost exactly where I left him and doesn't seemed surprised at all that I've returned when I throw open the door. He doesn't rush to me to help me with my jacket or to bow, but just stands there, my other baggage by his feet, looking at me with confidence. Suddenly everything becomes very clear to me.

"You bastard! What the fuck did you do to my flight, to my vacation, to my life!"

"Maîtresse, please let me take care of you," he begins, but I cut him off quickly.

"Take care of me? This is kidnapping! You do not, I repeat, you do not have a right to keep me here!" I yell at him.

Out of the corner of my eye I see the man who was at the auction and who visited the suite step out of the kitchen. "Mademoiselle, I can explain everything to you, but you must calm down," he says with a heavy accent. He turns to Philippe. "You need to be dressed properly," he says simply as he tosses him a bag. "As do you, Mademoiselle," he adds to me.

"I'm staying in my own clothes, so you can just tell me what is going on!"

The stranger sighs and holds up his hands. It is at this moment that I notice two other men by the front door. Clearly this is a nightmare coming true. I can see the headlines now: Erotica Author Held Captive. "The first duty of every captive is to escape" is something I heard in a history class once, but I don't think they were talking about being trapped on another planet. I'm not one of my heroines, so I decide to go along with this for a while.

Philippe disappears into the bedroom and emerges a few minutes later dressed in long pants and a shirt with a jacket over it. He looks very much the gentleman except for the open collar and the metal ring around his neck. The stranger says something angrily to him, and Philippe just tosses the necktie on the floor. He walks to me and kneels down, offering me his leash.

The stranger swears and gives an order to the other two. The leash is placed in my hand, then I'm escorted out of the suite and into a carriage. Philippe is sitting next to me, so I scoot over as far as the seat allows, dropping the leash and folding my arms across my stomach, refusing to look at him. The stranger, clearly in charge of this crime, is sitting in the other seat with one of the two guards. The other guard is sitting with the driver on top.

For a while everything is silent, and then the stranger begins speaking in very calm-sounding tones to Philippe. I can't understand it all, but apparently Philippe isn't an employee but the son of an important man, a man who is angry that his son is the slave of an American woman. "Look, I just thought he was an employee, you know, part of the fantasy of the place?" I say suddenly.

"You understand French?" the stranger asks, his eyes shocked.

"A little; I took it in college," I add. "Listen, I don't want to cause family problems, so why don't you just turn this thing around and find me a seat on the shuttle back to Earth? I'll forfeit the rest of my winnings."

"It is not that simple, Mademoiselle," the stranger says.

When I press for further information the stranger just tilts his hat over his eyes and pretends to go to sleep. I lean back in the seats and hold up one hand when Philippe starts to speak. "I'm not going to listen to any more of your lies," I simply say. At this point my stomach is so tight in anger that his tears have no effect at all on me.

I refuse to kneel, and even though the king frowns he waves the guards away. Good thing too, since Philippe immediately placed himself between them and me. The king may not be happy with his son playing the role of a slave, but he doesn't want him hurt. Unless I have that wrong as well.

Philippe the Thirteenth is a direct descent of the founder of this planet, I'm told by the stranger, who I now know is one of the king's top men, the former tutor of the prince. Of course there follows the boring details of how disenfranchised the French had become after the European Commonwealth was established and how they were forced to flee or see their culture destroyed. Most of it is crap. Most of the French stayed on Earth and have adapted quite nicely to the changes; in fact, the tourist trade is better now than it was a century ago when these malcontents left. True, the language has all but disappeared, but the high fashions are still created there and it's the place to honeymoon.

But I know all this already, so I'm watching Philippe the Fourteenth closely. A prince. No wonder he was a bit clueless and yet so cultured in his behavior. He's watched slavery all his life, dreamed of it for himself, fully aware that here at least it isn't some consensual game. That is the truly scary thing for me – the fact that according to their law, I own him.

I blink a few times, then hold up one of my hands. "Would you please repeat that last part?"

"He is the heir, and therefore, by our law, you own the planet through him," the tutor repeats with that disapproving look.

"That's insane," I say. I smile at the king and take two steps toward him before the guards block my way. "Your Majesty, I'm just a writer from Earth, here on vacation. I had no idea who this person was." I motion toward the prince, who has hurried to my side and is eyeing the guards carefully. "I'm really sorry all of this happened, and I understand this is important to you, so I'll be willing to take the rest of my vacation now to help your son sort through his feelings."

The king speaks to me, and then the tutor interprets. "His Majesty says that it is far more serious than you realize. You will inherit the planet; as much shame as this brings to our people, it is nothing compared to the shame of his son's being a slave without an owner. You are far less dangerous than Count Domen. His Majesty insists that you stay here."

"This is kidnapping! Unless you show me some law that I've broken, I demand that you release me!" I'm still yelling when the guards escort me from the throne room.

I scream, kicking at the guards as they forcibly escort me to a suite, and then I pound on the door after they lock it. After a few minutes I calm myself and look at where I've been placed. Its not a dungeon, at least, though it is still a prison. I stalk over to the big bed and sit down. The cover is soft and probably silk or satin. There is no doubt in my mind that everything that looks expensive is indeed so.

Half an hour later the door opens, and Philippe enters with my luggage and some extra bags and boxes. "Maîtresse, I have brought your possessions," he says softly. Looking at him, once more dressed in the clothes of the slave class, I understand that he is including himself.

I stand up and walk to him. My slap surprises him so he can do no more than fall mutely to the floor, staring up at me in shock. "I don't give a damn if you're the king of the universe; you had no right to manipulate me like this!" I take one of my bags and stomp back to the bed. As I sit down the tears finally begin. I feel like I'm losing it, and I don't really care anymore.

"Mademoiselle Jackson," he says as he approaches me, and my surprise at the sound of my name makes me look up. "Oh, I did not mean to cause this," he says as he kneels by me and touches one of the tears on my cheek.

"Well, folks get a bit upset when they are denied their freedom," I retort, sniffing the tears back and pulling away.

"But in your stories," he begins.

"Stories! That's right – stories. Fiction, not reality!" Now it's starting to make a bit of sense to me. This poor kid grew up in a world where he was told to be master and had feelings of wanting to submit. All he had were the books he must have collected, apparently many of mine, which shouldn't surprise me, since my work is very popular.

"There are fantasies, like the resort says, and then there are realities," I try to explain. I use simple words in my attempt to convince him this is all a mistake. "You feel things that just don't click with your society. Then you read books, almost all of them set in high-fantasy worlds with perfect people giving and taking without repercussions. But real life has repercussions, Philippe. Especially when you're a prince."

He sits down on the floor and places his hands over his head for a moment. When he looks up his eyes are rimmed with tears. Even now I want to take that pain from him and push him in other directions, curing the past with firm loving control. "Mademoiselle Jackson," he begins slowly, "my father will not allow you to leave, and for this I am truly sorry. He will insist that you come out on state occasions and act as my owner; he will hide you away until he is dead. Then I will let you go and accept whatever comes."

He stands up and starts to leave when I block his way. "Will you?"

"Yes, of course, Mademoiselle," he says. I see the hunger in his eyes, though lined with deep sadness.

I let him go then and think about my current situation. My life on Earth is hollow, really. Oh, the fact that I'm well-known to almost everyone is a drag. Fame shows itself first in the number of people who love you, and I've had hundreds claim that, and second in the number of people who hate you or are jealous of you, and there have been thousands of those. And the fact remains that none of my relationships work out. Doomed to be a straight dom woman in a world either opposed to the dom woman part or opposed to the straight part, I had few friends and even fewer lovers.

I look in the mirror. At the age of thirty what did I have other than my awards and my writing? And here I was literally being offered the figurehead of a planet. Well, that sounds better, but it still doesn't sit right, so I consider my options some more.

I fold my arms across my stomach and wait for my bombshell to explode in their minds. It's morning, and right after breakfast I demanded to see the king. I got right to the point. I'll stay, but under certain conditions. Oh, and don't try to force me; I'll just not cooperate at all, and then their world and those they get tourists from will see what a sham this whole setup is.

Amazingly, the king listened and only swore a few times during my rehearsed speech. If I have to stay here, I refuse to be a mere figurehead. I want some concessions from them, and in return I'll be a good mistress for Philippe and even consider making sure another heir is available. I haven't had kids yet, and the prince out-shines most other men I've known. And I'll get to keep writing, so I'll need all my things from Earth.

The tutor relays the fact that the king has agreed to my conditions and asks if there is anything else.

"Yes; if this is going to happen, I want it done right. You must have ceremonies for this kind of thing." The king scowls at this. "Look, your people already know, and if not, Count Domen is well on the way to telling them. From what your son tells me, the count won't portray me as anything less than a threat to this place, to your culture. You make a public announcement of this and you cut his threat off at the base."

The king nods. I'm informed that the ceremony will take place in a month so that I'll have time to learn the courtly manners and a bit more of the planet's history. I agree and ask if I may invite some guests. The king rolls his eyes, not cherishing the thought of more pushy Terrans in his palace.

Epilogue: Two Months Later

I must keep myself from smiling too much as my guests from Earth approach the thrones. Sitting next to the king, to his right in a smaller version of his throne, has become comfortable for me since agreeing to stay here. Philippe the Thirteenth has turned out to be a very nice man, almost like a kind grandfather. He adopted me formally a few weeks ago, but this festival will publicly declare me his heir and partly confirm the rumors that have been circulated by Count Domen. Though not in the way I'd dreamed of, I have married a prince; that was part of the ceremony of adoption. I reach down to where my slave prince is sitting by my feet and tousle his hair as my guests stop before the thrones.

I've only asked the ones I was closest to on the council back in Manhattan, and my editor Bryan. I rise to my feet, as does my slave prince, and bow to the king. My colleagues follow me silently out of the throne room and through the hallways to the set of suites that have been readied for them.

"Is this for real?" Duane asks once the doors have been closed behind us.

"No way," Angie says as she watches Philippe prepare drinks for everyone. I told him what everyone's favorite was, so he doesn't speak or even look at them. "I mean, he can't be a prince," she continues.

"I haven't lied to you," I simply say as I sit down on one of the straight-backed chairs. The skirts needed for formal occasions, such as greeting anyone in the throne room, make sitting in anything more comfortable impossible. I've started to realize how much freedom my slave prince has gained and how much I've lost as these weeks have rolled by. Yet I've gained much more as well, his eyes tell me as he bows and gives me my ginger ale.

"It's like one of your stories – hell, several of your stories," Bryan states. He takes the drink with a bit of a blush. Though a great editor, he himself isn't a player at all, just an admirer, I think, who never had the guts to go beyond the books he worked on.

"So may I ask him?" Janet asks. She and I had become close via the signings I did at her clubs. Had I been attracted to women at all, I would have had her on her knees. In many ways, she reminds me now of a female version of Philippe as she takes the drink from him, her eyes wide in wonder and desire.

"Philippe, feel free to speak to my friends," I instruct. Was that a royalist arch in my voice I just heard? I think I rather like it if it was, especially the way it causes Philippe to bow to me again.

"So, you're really a prince, the heir to this whole planet?" Janet asks as she takes her drink, white wine with a twist of lemon.

"Yes, Ma'am," Philippe says. He pauses, waiting for her to speak again, but she just blushes and walks toward me slowly. He offers Duane his drink, Scotch on the rocks.

"So why would you give all this power and wealth up?" Duane asks. I know that he can't imagine anyone giving up such things himself, since he has had to struggle every day with paying his rent back home. He almost didn't accept this trip because of his pride, but it's that pride, the real pride in himself, that makes him a good man, a great master to the select women he has. In his voice I sense something I've rarely known Duane feel: envy, jealousy.

Philippe tilts his head to one side as he replies. "Sir, I would follow Maîtresse to the poor house. I have no need of power or wealth; I never had."

"So you always felt submissive?" Angie asks as she walks to them and takes her drink, a bloody Mary.

"Yes, Ma'am. Maîtresse says that there is a theory that such is possible," he offers. His English is getting better, but it isn't great yet, but then we've been using French most of the time so I won't embarrass everyone at the public introduction tomorrow.

Angie nods and steps back. She looks him up and down, then grins at me. "Damn, you get all the luck, Kimberly."

I smile now and stand up. "I must leave you now. We all must rest. The ceremonies and luncheons, and then the dinners, will be tiring. I hope you all can enjoy your stay," I say in very formal language.

Then I open my arms and give them each a hug as I'm leaving. To each I whisper my hopes that they too can enjoy a similar experience. I will tell them of this arrangement later, after it is clear that I have been accepted here by all the people.

It will be a few months, but the agreement the king and I signed states that the borders will be opened and the prices lowered. There are too many people here suffering for another person's fantasy and too many back on Earth yearning for one beyond their reach. The key is to submerse yourself in the fantasy. And am I not now the mistress of fantasy and reality in this place?

a note from the author

WHEN I BEGAN THIS BOOK I HAD TWO principal goals. First, to write a follow-up to the title story of my first erotica collection, "Punishment for the Crime." I heard many of you were distressed by the ending of the story. (Yes, I intended from the beginning to write "Justice" anyway.) Second, to write down the interesting and arousing stories that harassed me day and night. My creations tend to be very demanding of my time. In a very real way, a writer bottoms to her creative talents and submits to the worlds forming in her mind. Speaking with other writers I've discovered this to be true for the majority of us.

After reading over all the stories in this book, however, I discovered two covert themes, perhaps even unconscious goals of mine. The themes are complexity and choice. In each story the characters must make choices based on what they want and who they are, choices influenced heavily by the complexity of the situation and the people around them. The question is asked over and over: Is anything easily attained really worth having?

Reflecting, I see that I personally just realized this myself and as a result am far happier in all ways than I was before. Oh, my heart still gets stomped on and I find the duds still but that is less frequently than it used to be. When the negative happens I cry and rant and get very angry, and then I hope I can learn from the experience and more on to another set of choices. Choices determined by figuring out what I want and by my previous decisions – just like my fictional characters in this collection.

How many of you readers saw these themes: complexity and choice? If you didn't, or if the knowledge that my work is deeper than simple sexual frustration and fulfillment now leaves you concerned, don't worry. Like I said, I didn't realize it either until the stories were finished; most of my time was spent enjoying the sensual fantasies, wishing I could be in that female character's position.

Every major character, especially the women, contains part of myself, some more than others, both the good and the negative traits. I think this is true for most authors I've spoken with or read anything about. This doesn't mean that everything I write about turns me on, however, nor that I'd want to do everything I write about. Some things are realistic and others are non-consensual, where I draw my own personal limits.

This collection was for you to enjoy, not a manual for how you should scene or what you should fantasize about. Turning you on is an erotic power rush for me, but tickling your mind is a thrill as well. So, tell me: did I do both?

Two final words of thanks. To Janet Hardy of Greenery/Grass Stain Press, the publisher, for making it possible for all of you to share my work. To Tom, my husband, the first man in my life, the first person in my life, my strength and my support. I love you, Tom.

Tammy Jo Eckhart
December 1998

Other Books from Greenery Press and Grass Stain Press

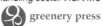